A BEGINNER'S GUIDE TO RULING THE GALAXY

OUT OF THIS WORLD REVIEWS FOR
MY BROTHER IS A SUPERHERO

"I even think my dad would like reading this book!"
David, The Book Squad, The Beano

"Cosmic! Amazing! Outstanding! Probably the funniest book
I have read for a long time."
Alison A. Maxwell-Cox, The School Librarian

"I was so addicted to it that my mum had to make me put it down."
Calum, aged 11

"Funny, fast moving and deftly plotted, it's the best thing to hit
the superhero world since sliced kryptonite."
Damian Kelleher, Dad Info

"You know a book is going to be good when you're giggling after
five minutes… Ideal for comic readers and superhero experts."
Nicola Lee, The Independent

"An excellent adventure story with real heart that's also properly
funny."
Andrea Reece, Lovereading4Kids

"You'll laugh until you fall out of your tree house!"
Steve Coogan

"A brilliantly funny adventure with twists, turns, crazy characters
and a really hilarious ending. Fantastic!"
Sam, aged 11

"Brilliantly funny."
The Bookseller

A BEGINNER'S GUIDE TO RULING THE GALAXY

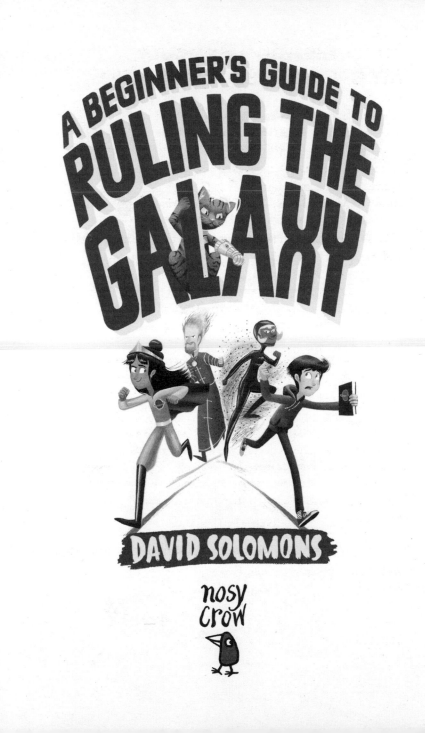

DAVID SOLOMONS

nosy crow

First published in the UK in 2022 by Nosy Crow Ltd
The Crow's Nest, 14 Baden Place,
Crosby Row, London, SE1 1YW, UK

Nosy Crow Eireann Ltd
44 Orchard Grove, Kenmare,
Co Kerry, V93 FY22, Ireland

Nosy Crow and associated logos are trademarks and/or registered
trademarks of Nosy Crow Ltd

ISBN: 978 0 85763 993 6

A CIP catalogue record for this book is available from the
British Library.

Printed and bound in the UK by Clays Ltd, Elcograf S.p.A.
Typeset by Tiger Media

Papers used by Nosy Crow are made from wood grown in sustainable forests

MIX
Paper from
responsible sources
FSC® C018072

3 5 7 9 10 8 6 4 2

www.nosycrow.com

For Luke and Lara

Chapter 1

"I claim this adequately rated secondary school in the name of the Galactic League!"

Puzzled to hear such an odd declaration, Gavin looked up to see a tall girl with long black hair standing on the top step outside the main entrance of Middling High, hands on her hips, chin jutting out, addressing the milling playground like some junior dictator. The morning sun gleamed off the buttons on her uniform blazer, her dark eyes shone and her hair streamed in the breeze. A discarded crisp packet blew by, briefly catching on her foot. Gavin didn't recognise her and, despite the impressive display, no one was paying her the slightest

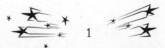

attention. No one except for him. The girl turned on one heel and marched over.

It was just before the bell went for the start of classes and he was sitting on the far side of the steps reading a book, on his own as usual. The girl seemed to have some difficulty focusing on him at first, but eventually her gaze landed and suddenly he felt like a specimen under a microscope.

"Your skin," she remarked. "It's so ... pale." She rolled up one sleeve and stuck her arm next to his. The contrast between her sandy complexion and his pasty skin was striking. "Remarkable. You're almost translucent. Not a friend to the ultraviolet end of the spectrum, I'm guessing. Good job this planet only has one sun."

Assuming that this was her awkward attempt at saying hello, Gavin ignored the general weirdness of the comment. He hadn't seen her at school before and since he had plenty of experience of being the new kid, he decided to give her a break.

He lowered his book. "So, do you always go around claiming schools for – what was it again?"

"The Galactic League," she repeated in a tone of voice that suggested she was disgusted he hadn't heard of it.

Her accent marked her out as not from around here, so

he figured it must be some foreign football league. Still, an odd comment to make, even for an ardent fan. "I'm Gavin, by the way."

"Gavin?" she said, intoning his name like she'd just discovered a new species of frog. "*The* Gavin?"

He was the only one in Year 8. There was another in Year 12, but everyone called him Shed, because once he'd got locked in his dad's garden shed over a bank holiday weekend and had to survive on birdseed and spring water from a four-pack of canned tuna. He hadn't eaten the tuna because he couldn't find any mayo. So, yes, Gavin supposed that made him *the* Gavin, whatever that meant.

The girl put a hand over her right eye and squinted at him with her left, her eyeball circling wildly. "So it's true. It's like you're barely here."

"Fine," he said, losing interest and burying his head in his book. His plan was to ignore her until she went away. But then he noticed a boy tearing across the playground with a stiff, upright running style, arms pumping, knees somewhere around his ears. The boy carved a path through clumps of kids, heading towards the main entrance.

"There you are," he said to the girl, trotting up the steps. He was slightly shorter than she was, an athletic

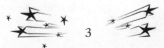

body topped by a disproportionately big head. "You wandered off," he continued. "Sam – I mean, *Dad* – told you not to leave my side, at least for our first day."

So they're brother and sister, thought Gavin. Maybe twins.

She glowered and he shrank from her. "No one orders me about. Especially not some hairy warrior."

"Some what?" said Gavin.

The boy let out a startled cry, evidently just noticing him sitting there. He sent Gavin a nervous glance and began to honk like a goose. "*Worrier*. Dad's such a worrier." The boy paused for a moment. "And he is hairy." He raised a hand in greeting. "I'm Bart," he mumbled, and then added, "I come in peace."

Oh no, not another one. "Good for you," said Gavin. "I came on my bike."

The boy frowned. "That is an example of comedic wordplay, correct?"

Gavin was coming to the surprising conclusion that the boy might be even weirder than his sister. "Sure. You a big fan of comedic wordplay, Bart?"

The boy and girl exchanged a puzzled glance. "Ye-e-s," he said slowly, "I am *Bart*. That is correct. Because 'Bart' is a statistically commonplace designation."

"Nice to meet you," he said, even more keen to get

back to his book and far away from these two. "I'm Gavin."

"*Gavin?*" The boy's eyes widened. "Is he the one?"

The girl ignored him. "What's that?" she asked, referring to Gavin's Spork of the Dead-themed lunchbox.

Unsure if she hadn't recognised the greatest video game in the world, or a basic packed lunch box, he didn't answer at first. She took it as an invitation to investigate further.

"Hey!" he objected as she removed his sandwiches and took a large bite.

"Oh, mmm," she gushed. "It's so utterly, incredibly … *bland*. I don't think I've ever tasted anything so wholly *unremarkable* in my whole life. What is it?"

"Uh … cheese and ham," said Gavin, looking around the playground for the telltale smirks on the faces of his schoolmates that would signal this was a prank.

"*Uh-Cheesinam,*" she repeated in wonder, staring at the sandwich as if it was the Crown Jewels, before tearing off another chunk.

Gavin found his tongue. "That's my lunch you're eating."

She waved away his concern. "I'll have one of the servants prepare you a fresh Uh-Cheesinam. Or perhaps you'd prefer something more interesting – how about

a slice of Tilorthian Phlan? Your taste buds will think you've died and gone to Alpha Centauri."

Bart began to honk again, as if his sister had cracked the funniest joke. "Isn't she a hoot? *Phlan? Servants? Earth's closest planetary system?* I ask you, as if a perfectly normal human schoolgirl would have *staff* and an intergalactic packed lunch."

"So." She gave a long sigh and flicked her hair. "What is there to do here?"

"At school?"

"No. In this habitat."

Strange word to use. "You mean Middling?"

"If that's how its inhabitants refer to their environment."

If she was hoping for bright lights and a world-class aquarium, she'd come to the wrong *habitat*. Gavin had lived in Middling since he was nine years old, which made a running total of three years, four months, two weeks, and five days. He'd had a lot of different homes over the years, so he liked to keep count. He muttered something about it being a nice spot to live, if a little quiet.

"Apple," she said.

"No, it's grapes today." He pulled out a bunch of seedless South Africans from his lunchbox.

"I refer to my personal designation," she said. Gavin gave her a blank look and she curled her lip in frustration before clicking her fingers. "Name!" She said it like she'd produced a rabbit from a hat. "My name is Apple." She paused. "Niki Apple."

"Cheesely," he said. "Gavin Cheesely."

"You have my condolences," said Niki.

The bell went for the start of school. The kids in the playground lumbered zombie-like up the steps and in through the main entrance. When the crowd thinned, Niki and Bart had gone. For a moment, Gavin wondered if he'd imagined the two of them, but then they strolled back through the open doors on to the steps. Even his imagination wasn't strange enough to conjure up these two.

"What are you waiting for?" said Niki. "As I understand from my briefing, the repetitive sound of the directly struck idiophone percussion instrument—"

"She means the bell," Bart added hurriedly.

Niki pursed her lips, swatting him away like a persistent fly. "The *bell* signifies the commencement of training. Oh, I do hope the first class is hand-to-hand combat. I have sharpened my nails especially."

She disappeared inside with an eager bounce and what Gavin judged to be a frankly disturbing look in her eye.

Bart paused. "I know what you're thinking," he said. "That she's cruel and uncaring and only interested in herself."

Gavin waited for the next half of the sentence, the bit where Bart went on to explain that really she's not like that at all, and how once you got to know her she was kind and gentle and actually a great big softy.

It didn't come.

"Bart, attend me this instant!" Niki's piercing tone blasted out of the entrance like a high-explosive round.

Bart winced and, with one final apologetic look towards Gavin, trotted after her. "Coming, Your High—" He broke off. "I mean … coming, regular biological sister."

Closing the book, Gavin stuffed it and the remains of his lunch into his bag and prepared to head to his first class. If he'd known then what he would later learn, what he should've done was drop everything, hightail it in the opposite direction, change his name to Jose Silva and immediately relocate to Brazil. But at that precise moment he had no idea that though Niki Apple had only just appeared in his life, she was about to make quite an impact.

Like that asteroid did on the dinosaurs.

Chapter 2

Deciding that Niki was a fruitcake with extra crazy currants, Gavin made every effort to steer clear of her after that. However, she had different ideas. Even when he thought he'd given her the slip, he would turn a corner or open a classroom door and there she'd be, popping up like an incredibly insulting jack-in-the-box, Bart trailing her every step. He didn't know why she was so keen to accompany him both in and out of school, and whenever he asked, she invariably changed the subject. In one incident a few months after their first meeting, he'd accused her of spying on him with a pair of binoculars, which she vehemently denied, claiming

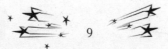

instead to be an innocent bird-spotter. An explanation that would've been more believable had they not at the time been standing in the queue for McDonald's.

Gavin considered that the attention from Niki wouldn't have been so bad if she'd been in any way, shape or form ... pleasant. But that was not the case. *Reserve my table at luncheon, reserve my place in art class, reserve my seat on the bus* – there was an awful lot of reserving.

"Entitled, that's the word," he confided to Bart in a quiet moment between slights. They were in biology with Mr Chetty. At least here he had some respite from her, sitting on the opposite side of the room. Not that Bart was a great improvement over Niki. He was one of those people whose life consisted of exercise and salad (Gavin had never seen him with so much as a packet of Fruit Pastilles). Perpetually happy, he was an advert for a clean-living, healthy lifestyle. And, honestly, he was a bit annoying – though not half as much as his sister. "She's so arrogant," Gavin griped. "I mean, some people act like they're better than everyone else, but usually they're covering for the fact that they're lacking in confidence. Niki's not like that. You look into those eyes and you can tell that she utterly *believes* she's top banana."

Bart nodded sagely. "I hadn't appreciated that the banana was so revered in your culture. Then again,

who could resist its potassium-rich, curvy, squishy yellowness – am I right?"

Gavin regarded him with a mixture of confusion and sympathy. "I can't imagine being her brother."

"No," agreed Bart. "Must be dreadful." He caught Gavin's expression, quickly cleared his throat and nodded again. "I mean, yes, *dreadful*. The entitlement. The arrogance. The bananas."

Mr Chetty instructed the class to choose partners for the next experiment. Before Gavin knew what was happening, Niki had marched over, ejected Bart from his chair and claimed Gavin for her partner. She flopped down next to him and swept her gaze round the class.

"So which one is to be dissected?" she asked in a bored voice.

"Beg pardon?"

"We are studying anatomy, yes?" She cast an imperious look over her classmates. "Then which one of these specimens do we cut up?" Her eyes brightened with excitement. "Or do we get to choose? If so, I pick Audrey Woods. Although overweight, the pallor of her skin suggests healthy internal organs that would prove suitable for study. So is there an operating table in the stationery cupboard or do we slice her open here?"

"You know I can hear you, right?" said Audrey, who

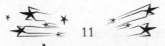

11

was sitting at the next desk.

"We don't do live animal dissections in this country any more," said Gavin. "Perhaps in your old school...?"

Niki nodded with understanding and in a matter-of-fact voice said, "What you need is a specimen that would welcome being dissected. Bart?"

"Right away!"

Bart sprang from his seat, charged to the front of the class and offered himself up for scientific study. It took a surprising amount of persuasion for Mr Chetty to convince him that under no circumstances was he about to slice open a student. The remainder of the hour passed without further incident, but Gavin found himself watching Niki with renewed bafflement. And yet for all her strangeness – or perhaps because of it – he was aware that the other kids in school were spellbound by her. Sometimes it felt to him like Niki was riding atop a glorious, rainbow-coloured carnival float, waving regally at a vast crowd, lit by her own personal ray of sunshine, while he was standing by the side of the road holding a stick of candyfloss, watching her go by. In the rain.

◆

Gavin walked home from school alone. It was one of the few times he could count on not being harassed by Niki. While he liked nothing better than to leave at

the end of the school day, she crammed her week with every possible after-school activity. Chess club, martial arts, debate team and pottery, to name but a few; she possessed a competitive spirit that compelled her to pit herself against everyone and anyone. Even her ceramic sheep were aggressive. He reached his house on Park Street and turned into the driveway. If eluding Niki in school was hard, doing so at home was even harder, since she lived in the house next door. As soon as the Apples had moved in a few months ago, their driveway became a procession of nosy neighbours bearing casseroles and questions. But to the frustration of the street, and with the exception of Niki's relentless pursuit of Gavin, the Apples kept themselves largely to themselves.

Unlike his house, Niki's had an upper floor and the top window with the star-patterned curtains was her bedroom. He knew that she wouldn't be home yet – it was music practice today and she was first violin in the orchestra. Apart from a few odd facts like these, it struck him that he didn't know much about her. He knew even less about her family. He had briefly met Mercedes, her mum, when she'd invited him over for what she called a "typical human lunch". She served jam sandwiches, which turned out to be a slice of chicken squeezed between layers of strawberry jam. Her dad, Sam, was just as odd. One Saturday morning Gavin had been in his back garden, which bordered the Apples', when through the fence that divided them he'd heard Niki's mum and dad talking.

"Have you got any dark stuff?" Mercedes had asked.

Sam hadn't answered at first, leaving a thoughtful pause during which Gavin stuck his eye to a small hole in the fence, to see the long-haired Sam looking past Mercedes with a thousand-yard stare.

"I've seen things," Sam had muttered. "Terrible things. Attack ships on fi—"

"No," Mercedes had interrupted him. "*Dark* stuff. I'm putting a wash on."

As eccentric as the other Apples were, it was Niki who took the biscuit. Actually, she didn't take it so much as terrify it out of its wrapper and crush it to dust in her triumphantly aloft fist. Gavin stuck his key in the door. He had a strong suspicion that she was hiding something. Other people would be desperate to know what, but not him. He preferred to keep his head down and get on with his life. Whatever Niki was keeping secret, he was certain of one thing.

It had nothing to do with him.

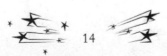

Chapter 3

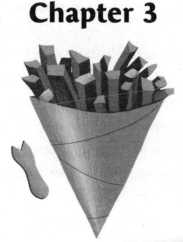

Niki lay back on her bed with a deep sigh of satisfaction. Orchestra practice had gone particularly well this afternoon. Mr Warble the music teacher had remarked that he'd never seen a violin used like that. Well, it was Tanisha Day's own fault – she shouldn't have come in early on the second bar. She gazed up at the swaying shadows on her sloping ceiling. She'd commandeered this bedroom as soon as they moved in. It was the biggest in the house, although its size paled in comparison with the grand living spaces to which she was accustomed. She sighed. She missed her old life. Well, not all of it, but definitely the simple things – like a massive luxury

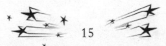

suite with its own spa, private zoo and a convertible roof. Sam had objected to her taking the upper storey of the house, saying it was harder to defend from attack or infiltration. Such a bore. He would have preferred her to sleep in a more secure location. She tutted to herself. The background research she'd been supplied with before their arrival in Middling had included a sample of typical fiction, including one genre of story that seemed exclusively to involve young women – often women of rank with great hair – being locked up in towers by their elders. Sam would approve. Were it up to him, she would be bolted behind a two-metre-thick Teledium metal door in some subterranean prison. Without her hair straighteners.

There was a hesitant knock at the door.

"Go away," she called out in irritation. Hadn't she made it clear to the rest of the Apples that she was not to be disturbed? Having to spend so much time at Middling High School was wearing. School wasn't taxing intellectually or physically, of course; she was far smarter and more able than anyone else there, including the teachers. No, it was the tedium of this existence that she needed to take time out of, and in particular the task she'd been set by Sam and Mercedes, which was a wearisome burden. Following that unremarkable neighbour boy

everywhere felt like the biggest waste of her time. Be his shadow, Sam had insisted. She understood why he wanted her to stick to Gavin, but that didn't mean she had to like it. Or him. She swung her legs off the bed and stood up, then reached in the gap between her mattress and bed frame and pulled out a sleek mobile phone. Its bright casing shimmered like it had been carved from a cloud using a sliver of ice.

There was a gasp from the door. She whirled round to see Bart standing there, his anxious gaze trained on the phone.

"Do Mum and Dad know you've got that?"

"They are *not* my mum and dad. And they're never going to find out," she said, adding darkly, "Are they?"

"No. Never," he gulped. "Uh, so what are you using it for, exactly?"

"What on Earth?"

"I said, what are you using—"

"No." She rolled her eyes. "It's the title of my channel." She turned the phone around so he could see the screen. On it was an image of a smiling Niki, just about recognisable beneath a ton of filters, above which was splashed the phrase "What on Earth?"

He squinted at the screen. "Why's there a number six there?"

17

Niki snatched the phone away and sniffed. "That's my followers."

"Oh."

"I've just started," she said defensively. "Give it a month and a few irresistible posts and it'll be—"

"Seven?"

"Thousands!" She threw him a murderous look. "Millions!" She strutted into the centre of the room. "If I'm stuck here, I might as well do something to entertain myself. Now, be silent." She swept back her hair took a deep breath and …

… her head burst into flames.

Instead of running about in panic looking for a fire extinguisher like any normal person would do under the circumstances, she just fixed a smile across her face. The flames encircled her head like a burning crown.

"You're not supposed to do that—" began Bart, immediately falling silent under her fiery glare.

"I will do exactly as I wish," she said coldly, pointing the phone at her face and tapping the record icon. "Dread Princess Xyllara, Spawn of D'Rek the Destroyer, Firelord of Trilia Zed Zed 6, Inheritor of the Haunted Stars, First Hatchling of Pamnatakrocula the Pitiless, Sovereign of Shadows, heir apparent to the throne of the Dark Galaxy, coming to you again from planet Dirt.

OK, so it's ... five-thirty in the evening of my ninety-second day in this desolate place. As bad as it is having to trail around after Gavin Cheesely like he possesses the secret of the ancients, it's made so much worse by taking place here. Its inhabitants refer to it as—"

"NO!" shouted Bart. "You're not supposed to say where we are!"

Niki's flames shot higher and she sent him a dangerous look.

"Sorry," he mumbled apologetically. "I just mean, it's not safe. Sam and Mercedes say—"

"I don't care what they say." She gave a dismissive tut. "And, anyway, who's going to find out? No one's going to come across this place, not in a million years. If there's a bright spot in the universe, then Middling is as far from it as a bold, independently minded Galactic League princess could possibly find herself." She returned her attention to the video. "On today's episode of 'What on Earth?' I want to talk about something that came up at orchestra practice today. And I don't mean Tanisha Day's bruise. No, I am referring to the four-beat musical combo known as Cubic Parsec, the most successful and sensational pop group on this planet, according to my classmates. I detect notable increases in heart rate and elevated skin temperature whenever the group is discussed, especially its lead singer, Hal Hill. The topic of conversation today was Cubic Parsec's major new tour. Obviously, they're not coming to Middling, and yet the excitement here is palpable. The unwarranted adulation for a glamorous figurehead I can totally understand." She wrinkled her nose. "It's the songs I don't get. 'Talkin' 'Bout a Pollution Revolution', 'Polar Bear Blues', 'It's the Climate, Mate'. They're all about what people here refer to as 'the environment'. By which they mean the air, earth, water and all the living things that surround them. Young people in particular are obsessed with 'the environment'. And not in the way you'd expect – they want to *protect* it. I know. You'd think it was the only planet they had. The inhabitants of this place have no idea how to conduct themselves like a civilised culture. Haven't they read *Ruling the Galaxy – A Guide for the Aspiring Tyrant?*" She snapped her fingers and pointed to her bookcase. Bart hurried over, retrieved a large hardback book prominently displayed there and handed it to her. She balanced it on one knee and flicked through the pages. "Yes, here it is. Chapter twenty-three explains the importance of the environment. You extract as much as your machines can pull from the soil, the air, the oceans, then move on to the next world and start all over again. That's progress. That's conquest. That's how

you build *an empire!*"

Niki ended the recording with an indifferent swipe at the phone and waved Bart away. "You are dismissed."

Bowing low, he retreated to the door and hesitated, remembering why he had come in the first place.

"Why are you still here?" Niki demanded.

"Dad said I had to get you. It's time to leave for the quiz."

She yawned. "I've changed my mind. I'm not going."

"But you have to!"

She could see him regret his choice of words as soon as they slipped from his tongue. No one told her she *must* do anything, especially not someone like Bart.

"Apologies," he grovelled. "But people will ask questions if you don't show, and you know what Mum and D— Sam and Mercedes say about unwanted questions."

Let them ask their questions. She was fed up pretending. Fed up hiding her light. It was such a *blisteringly beautiful light!*

"It's the final," said Bart hopefully. "And it's against Middling Academy."

Middling Academy was Middling High's arch-rival. Now, that was a concept she could get behind: an adversary to defeat. An enemy to *crush*.

"Fetch my outer layer," she commanded, striding past him out of the bedroom and heading downstairs.

"And would you like a banana?" he said, tripping after her.

She frowned. "Why would I want a banana?"

"No reason," he said, reaching the foot of the staircase. He crossed the tiny hallway, plucked her coat from the stand and helped her on with it.

"Now bring my personal transport around to the front of the dwelling," she ordered.

"Right away, Your Highness."

She placed her hands on her hips and declared to no one in particular, "I shall ride my twenty-six-inch Carrera Vengeance junior mountain bike to the quiz where I will single-handedly smite Middling Academy and then we will have chips!"

There was just one thing Earth had to offer that Niki had found favour with during her time on the planet: a bag of hot chips from Act of Cod, the fish and chip shop on the high street. And those little sachets of ketchup. It wasn't much, but it was a start.

Chapter 4

It was several months later and the middle of the summer term. Gavin was heading to his English class when he came across a traffic jam in the corridor. Kids were backed up all the way to the drinking fountain, complaining at the delay. With sinking inevitability, he saw that Niki and Bart were the cause of the hold-up. Niki stood in front of the notice board, studying it intently, seemingly unaware of the surrounding clamour. Behind her, Bart swayed back and forth across the corridor, weighed down by a huge sculpture he was attempting to carry. Gavin recognised it from art class. The theme of this term's project was "images of perfection" so, naturally,

Niki had chosen to sculpt a life-sized version of herself.

Unable to balance the sculpture any longer, Bart tripped, launching the figure through the air. Gavin looked up just in time to see the monumental Niki flying directly at him.

"Oof!" The sculpture slammed into him, knocking him to the floor. He lay there for a few seconds, dazed, the other students altering course around him like ants faced with an obstruction.

"What is this?" Niki asked, still looking at the notice board.

He struggled to his feet. At first he thought she was checking out a flyer advertising auditions for this year's school drama production of *Fiddler on the Roof*, but then he saw her gaze was fixed on a different poster, inviting nominations for the school's student council election.

She screwed up her face and pronounced the word in three distinct syllables. "El-ec-tion?"

Gavin was about to explain when she held up a silencing hand. He hated it when she did that, which she did *a lot*.

"No, wait, don't tell me. Is it when you lure a xenomorphic intruder into the airlock of your interplanetary craft and then blast the creature into the cold, unforgiving vacuum of outer space to perish?" She

beamed at Gavin with an expression of self-satisfaction.

Bart uttered his usual hooting laugh of disbelief. *"Airlocks, interplanetary craft, explosive decompression!* As if an anonymous and unremarkable human schoolgirl would have any experience in the containment and elimination of endoparasitoid extraterrestrial species."

"Ejection," said Niki, clicking her fingers and muttering. "That was it."

Gavin narrowed his eyes at her. "An election," he began, "is when a group of people – like the population of a country, or in this case, a school – decides together by voting on who should represent them to make the big decisions about how to run things. The student council gets to decide on things like the theme for the end-of-term dance and menus for the canteen. So they're not that powerful. Though the chairperson gets a special parking space for his or her bike right in front of the main entrance."

"Privileged parking," repeated Niki with a faraway gleam in her eye.

How could she not know what an election was? "Don't you have them where you come from?" He lowered his voice. "Is it because your country is under authoritarian rule? Is there, like, a tyrannical dictator who's been in charge for decades and who fixes the elections to ensure

he stays in power?"

Niki snapped out of her daydream and put an arm around Gavin's shoulders, walking him off down the corridor. "Tell me more about this 'election fixing'..."

◆

Three weeks later, Niki was officially installed as Student Council Chair. Not only was she the first Year 8 to assume the position, but she did so by taking a record ninety-seven per cent of the vote. Her first act was to push through legislation to change her title to Supreme Leader in Perpetuity. She gave her inaugural speech at a lavish celebration party she threw for herself in the school hall, which it transpired she'd paid for using most of the student council's annual budget. But the canapés *were* delicious. Gavin retained doubts about the fairness of the election, but he couldn't question Niki's popularity, especially not after she had led the school to a stunning victory over Middling Academy in the Quiz of Champions earlier that term. The Academy had won it last year, and the year before that. Having made it through yet again to the final round, they'd been firm favourites to emerge triumphant once more. Middling High's appearance in the final had come as a surprise to every other school in the district, but none more so than to Middling High. Their winning run was due entirely to

Niki. In the end, the final wasn't a competition so much as a massacre. She steamrollered over the brightest and best that the Academy had to offer, despite some of her answers coming across as rather eccentric. For instance, she refused to accept the quizmaster's assertion that it would take around seven months for a spaceship to reach Mars, insisting that Mars wasn't even a parsec away and then yelling, "What kind of engine-tech are you people using – *steam*?"

Since then she'd won prizes at school for everything, out-sprinting the opposition on the track and out-throwing them on the field (and on the pottery wheel). And it wasn't just physical prowess that made her stand out. As well as her quiz success, she'd nabbed the lead in the school play, much to the clench-fisted fury of Tanya Cloister-Moore, who could act, sing and dance, but nonetheless couldn't compete with Niki's star power.

She had this way of persuading people to do just what she wanted. The whole school had fallen for her … charms? No, that wasn't the right word. It was as if she exerted a mysterious force on all who came within her orbit. People obeyed her, instinctively. She was all-star, all-the-rage and verging on all-powerful.

So, naturally, it was Niki he had to face in the class debate that day.

He was anticipating a bloodbath. Not literally, but in Mrs Caesar's English class you never knew. Mrs Caesar, like her ancient Roman namesake, enjoyed nothing more than pitting students against one another in gladiatorial combat. Thanks to health and safety, she wasn't actually permitted to make them fight each other to the death in sandy arenas using swords and tridents. But she did love a good argument. That afternoon they were debating the motion: *This House believes there must be intelligent extraterrestrial life somewhere in the universe.*

"Our galaxy has at least two hundred billion solar systems," Niki began confidently. "So it's extraordinarily unlikely that the only life is here on Earth."

Twenty-eight heads swivelled to face Gavin for his response. (Actually, twenty-seven to be exact, since Jeffrey Burke was still wearing a neck brace following a run-in involving an e-scooter and the outside wall of the PE block).

"The factors that came together…" he mumbled.

"Speak up, Gavin," commanded Mrs Caesar, signing with an upturned thumb.

He cleared his throat. "The factors that came together to cause life on Earth are so rare that even in a universe as big as ours there's little chance of them occurring again."

The debate rolled on and for the next fifteen minutes

Niki battered him with her perfectly constructed arguments. He glanced at the classroom clock, counting down the last minute of the debate. He had one final point to make.

"If there is life out there," he stuttered, "then surely some of the aliens would be smart enough to figure out how to cross the galaxy. In which case, why haven't they come and said hello?"

A mumble of agreement rippled around the classroom. Even Mrs C allowed herself a flicker of a smile.

To Gavin's astonishment, Niki was silent. Then he saw that she was looking out of the window, wide-eyed, at a shaggy, tiger-striped cat sitting there staring back.

"Ms Apple," said Mrs Caesar. "Do you have a rejoinder?"

Just as Gavin was beginning to think he'd scored a knock-out point, Niki roused herself and came back at him.

"Human beings share sixty per cent of their genes with the banana," she said. "Maybe these super-smart aliens don't think it's worth crossing vast interstellar distances to meet a bunch of talking fruit."

There was a buzz as the clock ran out. The debate – and class – was over. Game, set and match to Niki. She didn't hang around to shake hands. Not even pausing to

collect her schoolbag, she bolted for the door.

Ten minutes later Gavin was ambling home. He kicked at a stone, sending it skittering across the pavement and into the gutter. Niki was such a show-off, strutting around Middling High School like she'd been voted most popular girl in school. Which, he supposed, she had.

"GAVIN – STOP THAT CAT!"

He spun round to see Niki storming along the pavement behind the same tiger-striped cat she had been staring at through the classroom window.

Gavin, return my library books. Gavin, fetch me another slice of strudel. Gavin, stop that cat. Seriously, who died and made her queen of the world? Turning his back on her, he continued on his way.

The cat squeezed through the gap between the railings and bounded into the park. Niki didn't break stride as she vaulted the fence and hotfooted it after her quarry.

Why was she so intent on catching it? To answer the question, he knew he would have to follow her. A little voice in his head piped up, warning him that he should stop right now and go home, but curiosity got the better of him. He took a fateful detour through the park.

Chapter 5

Niki sprinted across the children's playground with a determined expression, the cat zigzagging ahead of her, tantalisingly out of reach. She jumped on to an empty swing, catching the top bar in both hands and launching herself across the play park and on to the spinning roundabout, provoking shrieks from the youngsters playing there. Centrifugal forces fired her through the bright afternoon air, over the heads of a young mother and her bawling twins, who gazed up at the strange, soaring girl and instantly fell silent. She overtook the bolting cat to land directly in its path, kicking up a puff of dust as she thudded down to earth.

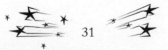

Seeing its escape route blocked, the cat dug its claws into the play-park surface and changed direction with the speed and agility of a toddler spotting an ice-cream van. It was running towards a familiar figure, standing there with all the dynamism of a traffic bollard.

"Gavin, grab it!" she yelled, but he just folded his arms. Why couldn't he follow a simple directive like any other obedient vassal? She watched as the cat shot across the park like a furry torpedo, not seeming to notice that Gavin lay directly in its path. It smacked into him and instinctively his hands clasped its wiry, wriggling body.

And then, suddenly, it stopped, becoming soft and still. With a sinuous stretch of its neck, it gazed up at him, opened its mouth. And spoke.

"You will pay for this, Earth boy."

Gavin's mouth opened and closed in speechless astonishment and he dropped the cat. It sped across the park, making for a small wooded area.

"Great," Niki groaned, tearing past him. "Couldn't even detain an unarmed cat." She flew after it into the trees. Pushing her way through a tangle of branches and brambles in an attempt to pick up its trail, she heard the snap of a twig from behind her and whirled round. It was only Gavin, breathing heavily, shock etched on his pale face.

"This is going to sound mad, but the cat," he hesitated, "it ... uh ... *talked*."

You'd think he'd never met a talking quadruped before. Then she remembered that these earthlings hadn't made it beyond their own moon and still believed they were the only sentient beings in the universe. Planet Dirt by name; mud-heads by nature. "I've no time for your edge-of-the-galaxy provincialism," she snapped. "Tell me exactly what it said."

Gavin blinked. "That I would pay for this, and then it called me Earth boy."

"I knew it."

"Knew what? Niki, what's going on? Why are you chasing a talking cat?"

She threw up a hand and they came to a stop at the edge of a small clearing in the wood. There was no sign of the cat, but in front of them was a metallic object a little bigger than the playground roundabout. Sitting on three spindly metallic legs, with a domed section in the centre, it was distinctly saucer-shaped.

Gavin raised a trembling finger. "What is that?"

"What does it look like?" Earthlings were backward, but had he really never seen a flying saucer? "It's the creature's ship."

"Cats don't have spaceships," he said in a small voice,

his eyes wide and staring. "They have litter trays and fluffy mice on strings."

There was a hum of power, and daylight appeared between the base of the vessel and the ground. With a swirl of leaves, it began to rise into the afternoon sky, its landing struts retracting into its body. The craft reached the level of the tallest tree, whereupon the glinting hull shrugged off its metallic appearance and became as translucent as a jellyfish.

"What happened?" said a startled Gavin. "Where'd it go?"

Couldn't he see that the craft had activated stealth mode? Standard procedure to avoid detection. Just then there came a faint buzzing sound from the edge of the wood and she spotted a small, fast-moving object skimming over the treetops. A drone.

"Down!" Niki dropped to the floor of the wood, pulling Gavin with her. There was a searing flash and an explosion from overhead. A shock wave rippled through the trees, shaking leaves from the branches, and a few seconds later sizzling fragments of flying saucer mixed with drone sprinkled down about them like fiery blossom. When she judged that the fallout had finished, Niki stood up and brushed a burning piece of shrapnel off her collar as if it was a fuzzy piece of lint. Gavin

remained prone on the ground, whimpering.

"OK then," she said breezily. "See you at school tomorrow." With that, she struck off out of the clearing, heading back towards the path.

Gavin uncurled himself from his foetal position and called after her. "Wait!"

"What is it now?"

"Are you kidding?" He gestured expansively to the chunks of disintegrated flying saucer. "Hello?"

"Goodbye."

To her annoyance, he followed her out, clipping at her heels and firing questions at her as they crossed the park. She could see his primitive mind desperately trying to make sense of the encounter.

"You are being highly intrusive," she complained as they turned into Park Street.

"Says the girl who hasn't left me alone all term long!"

She considered her options. Her martial arts training had taught her how to incapacitate any individual up to three metres in height with fewer than eight limbs. But would it stop him from spewing awkward questions about what he'd seen? Deciding that, sadly, violence was not the answer, she carried on towards home. Gavin had barely paused for breath by the time they reached her house and Bart opened the front door. He'd already

changed out of his school uniform and into his athletic gear, in preparation for the 10k run he took every day at this time. He bounced on his feet, like a rabbit in trainers.

"Hiya, Gavin!" he beamed. "Great to see you, neighbour!"

He said it as if they'd been reunited after years of wandering lost in the Amazon, and not since fifth-period physics.

"Hi, Bart," Gavin muttered in reply.

Niki pushed past him into the hallway. She viewed Bart with the same importance in her life as the toaster. No, that was unfair; she very much enjoyed a warmed crumpet. Bart just grinned and gave a happy wave. With Gavin's stream of inconvenient questions not abating even for a second, they passed through the house, out of the kitchen door and into the back garden. Like all the houses in the street, Niki's had a small garden, fenced on three sides. The square of grass contained Bart's trampoline ("great aerobic workout, neighbour!") and a neat, colourful flower border that Mercedes tended with a passion. It was also the site of Sam's home office, which sat against the back fence, a glass and wood construction the size of a large garden shed.

Niki beckoned Gavin in and closed the door behind them. Inside the compact room was a desk neatly

arranged with pens and stationery; a keyboard, trackpad and blank computer screen; and in front of the window a scrappy pot plant. The ergonomically designed chair, where Sam would normally sit, was empty. There was a small bookcase against one wall, which at a glance appeared to be filled exclusively with books about the card game of contract bridge. The only other item that gave a clue to his character was an electric guitar propped on a stand next to a boxy amplifier. The guitar was red, with a silver flash like a lightning bolt. In Niki's opinion he wasn't a very good musician, but with his great golden mane of hair he resembled images of old-fashioned Earth rock stars she'd seen in her background research material.

"OK, the door is locked and no one can overhear," said Gavin. "Now, will you tell me what just happened?"

"All will be revealed," she said cryptically. She was lying, of course. In truth, nothing would be revealed, not to this earthling. However, it was important that he follow her, and she judged that the prospect of learning the truth would ensure that happened. If all went to plan, in a matter of minutes he wouldn't remember anything. She crossed silently to the window and slid aside the pot plant, revealing a handle embedded flush in the floor beneath. Prising it out she rotated it clockwise through

37

ninety degrees. There was a whir as a square section of the floor retracted, exposing a flight of steps down. "Follow me," she said.

Music pounded up through the hatch. Someone with a gravelly voice was singing about "Livin' on a Prayer". They descended a short flight of steps to a room twice the size of the office above. Screens lining the walls showed maps of Middling at different scales. There was a moving weather map and a live satellite image of Earth from space. A green radar display like something out of a submarine was making a soft beeping sound with every sweep of its electronic dial. On a workbench were more drones like the one that had slammed into the flying saucer, in various states of assembly.

Niki saw that Gavin was too flabbergasted to speak. Well, that was a relief. She turned to Sam at the far end of the room, sitting with his back to them, his shaggy hair spilling over the seat's headrest. He was studying a screen showing a video replay of the moment the saucer exploded, viewed from a camera attached to the drone.

"Odd. The ship shouldn't have disintegrated," he mumbled. "The drone was only meant to disable it."

"Forget that," said Niki, crossing to the workbench. "We have another problem."

She reached for a shelf above the half-built drones.

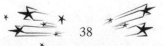

Propped on it was the incongruous form of an electric toothbrush. A label stuck beneath it read: *Danger! Not to be used to brush teeth.*

The castors of Sam's chair squeaked as he turned to face her and, as he did, his gaze fell on Gavin. He leapt up in surprise and with a toss of his luxuriant hair let loose a furious roar that shook the room.

Gavin gave a squeal of terror. Niki studied him with the curiosity of a scientist conducting a clinical trial. In the previous hour he had been threatened by a cat and rained on by an exploding flying saucer. And now he was witnessing this … transformation. She could see his meagre brain working at maximum power, and out of what she had no doubt was a whirling chaos of conflicting thoughts the last words that dribbled from his mouth before he slumped unconscious to the floor were:

"Your dad is … a lion?"

Chapter 6

Gavin woke up dazed and confused in the living room of the Apples' house, lying flat out on the sofa, surrounded by the curious faces of Niki and her family. On the mantelpiece a clock ticked reassuringly. The smell of dinner cooking drifted in from the kitchen. Everything seemed normal. Most importantly, her dad was no longer a lion, and for a moment he wondered if he'd imagined the whole thing. But then the events of the day flooded back to him and he sat bolt upright.

Before he could speak, Niki shoved an electric toothbrush in his face. There was a buzz and a whiff of spearmint as she pressed the button on the handle. The

head started spinning and he winced at the appearance of a dazzling green light.

"What do you remember?" she demanded.

The light faded as quickly as it appeared, but it had left a brush-shaped shadow on his vision. He blinked. "You mean, apart from the talking cat and the flying saucer?" His eye fell on Sam. "And your dad being the Lion King?"

Niki let out a cry of frustration, Bart buried his head in his hands and Sam snarled. Gavin felt as if he'd failed some test he didn't understand.

"Try it again," suggested Mercedes.

"It was already on maximum," Niki sighed. "It's not working on his brain."

"Brain?" said Gavin uneasily. "What kind of toothbrush is that?"

"Oh, just the regular Earth kind," said Mercedes with a kind smile.

"But the handle contains a powerful Obliterator engine and the head focuses the Erasure beam," Niki added.

Sam uttered a warning growl. "Princess, no…"

She ignored him and rattled on. "It wipes memories – or at least, it was meant to. Mercedes designed it to protect our true identities in case they were revealed to

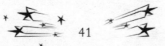

41

earthlings." She regarded the device with uncertainty. "Maybe there's a loose connection." She turned to Bart. "What's the capital of South Korea?"

"Uh ... Seoul?"

With a bored sweep of her hand, she aimed the toothbrush at him. The spearmint beam bloomed and faded as before.

"What's the capital of South Korea?" She repeated.

He looked at her blankly. "Half past three."

She turned to Mercedes. "No, it's working fine."

Gavin stood up sharply from the sofa. "You brought me back here so you could erase my memory!"

"Not all of it," Niki said with a carefree shrug. "Just this afternoon." She pursed her lips and blew out. "And anyway it didn't work."

"Right, that's it," said Sam. "We do this the old-fashioned way. He's seen too much, which means he's a threat. You know what we used to do with people like that, right?"

"We're not doing that," Mercedes said with a hint of exasperation.

"Absolutely not," agreed Niki.

Gavin breathed a sigh of relief. He didn't know exactly what Sam was referring to, but he was pretty sure he wasn't proposing a bottomless ice-cream sundae.

"I mean yes, of course, he's utterly insignificant," she went on. "But someone's bound to miss him." Then as an afterthought, she added, "Also, where would you get a High-Frequency Pain Disintegrator Cannon round here anyway?"

Gavin began to edge towards the door.

"Our security has been compromised," said Sam. "We have to do something about the boy." He stuck out a beefy arm, blocking Gavin's escape route, before gripping his collar and steering him back into the centre of the group. "Sorry. Nothing personal."

Gavin sent a cowed look round the faces of the Apples. What was happening here?

"I suspect the human brain is not complex enough for the sensors to register it as a threat," said Mercedes, examining the toothbrush. "I shall endeavour to improve the device's effectiveness."

"Very well, but what action do we take in the meantime?" said Sam.

"We could keep him here," said Bart, beaming at Gavin. "He could move into my room with me."

"Out of the question," said Sam.

"Well, he's not sharing mine," grumped Niki.

"He's not staying here at all!" Sam snapped. "I'm not sharing the bathroom with one more person."

"Then I can go?" said Gavin, sidling towards the door again.

"Not so fast." Sam's great arm grabbed him again, pressing him down on the sofa. "Since we have ruled out either elimination or abduction, you present an intractable problem."

"There is one remaining option," said Niki.

"Boiling in oil?" suggested Sam.

"Great suggestion, but no," said Niki. "I fear we have no other choice but to confide our secret in Gavin and trust him to keep it."

All four Apples turned their heads to stare at him.

"As the one in charge of your security, Highness," said Sam, "I must object to the sharing of any more classified information. No offence, Gavin."

"Uh ... none taken?"

Niki folded her arms. "But does he really pose much of a threat? I mean, what does it matter if we tell *him*? Who's going to believe Gavin?"

He felt the stinging barb of her insult, but no more than usual.

"Also, it will amuse me to observe his puny brain attempting to process the truth. After the day I've had, I could do with a laugh."

Sam relented with a low, grudging growl, before

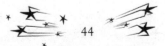

stomping over to an armchair and sinking into it to brood.

Mercedes chimed in with her assessment. "I calculate that there is a five per cent chance that Gavin's primitive brain will experience a catastrophic reaction to learning the reality of the situation."

Niki's eyes lit up. "You mean his head might explode?!"

Gavin looked desperately from one Apple to the other. Was this some kind of joke?

"Excellent," said Niki. "But I'm not cleaning up bits of brain off the carpet."

"Like you ever do any cleaning, *Your Highness*," Mercedes said tightly.

Gavin had heard enough. "Will one of you please tell me what's going on? Why did your mum call you Your Highness? Why was your dad a lion?" He stuck out an accusing finger. "And why did that cat talk?"

"The creature," said Niki. "It's not from here."

"Middling?"

She paused. "Earth."

Oh, come on! What utter nonsense. But Gavin's retort caught in his throat.

"And Sam is not a lion. Or a freelance technical copywriter. He's not even my real dad. He is a Leontine warrior, former commander of the Galactic

 45

League Honour Guard. And my guardian. In the course of everyday life on Earth, he uses a short-range concealment-field projector to hide his true form."

Head injury, was Gavin's first thought. He'd banged his head and was concussed, and all this was merely the ravings of his swollen brain. Or perhaps Niki had banged *her* head.

"Also, my name isn't Niki Apple."

"What is it then?" he asked.

"My full title is Dread Princess Xyllara, Spawn of D'Rek the Destroyer, Firelord of Trilia Zed Zed 6, Inheritor of the Haunted Stars, First Hatchling of Pamnatakrocula the Pitiless, Sovereign of Shadows, heir apparent to the throne of the Dark Galaxy."

She had lost it, big time. It couldn't be true. And yet. The cat, the flying saucer, the general oddness. His head was throbbing, and Mercedes seemed to sense his discomfort as she tucked a cushion behind his neck.

"You're saying that you're…" He looked around at their faces. "Aliens?"

"We prefer the term extraterrestrial," Mercedes said, plumping up the cushion. "Though technically I am what you would term an android."

Space-lions, galactic princesses, and her mum, who was not actually her mum, was a robot. Course she was.

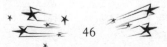

"My function within the group is to manage the princess's health and well-being, conducting medical intervention when necessary. Everything from the sniffles to major surgery." She held up an arm and her hand hinged at the wrist, revealing a cluster of built-in surgical instruments, ranging from scalpels to scissors. "Since Niki's anatomy and biology differ from a human being's, we cannot allow an Earth doctor to treat her or they would discover that she is not of this planet."

"My skin excretes a sweat-like compound that makes it safe from harmful UV light," Niki explained. "Which means I can sunbathe safely for *hours*. Also, I can utilise a natural pheromone that lets me influence weak-minded individuals and bend them to my will." She paused. "Oh yeah, and I have two hearts."

She might as well have said she had two heads. Gavin felt dizzy again.

"You OK, neighbour?" Bart's cheery face appeared in front of him like a shining sun. "Take some deep, cleansing breaths and you'll be fine." He began to demonstrate, inhaling and exhaling loudly.

"So ... if Niki's a princess," said Gavin, "then that makes you a prince, right?" Bart gave a snort and Niki stifled a laugh. "What'd I say? What's so funny?"

"I'm not her brother," said Bart. "We're not related

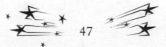

at all. My kind are grown in vats. I was created with the exact same blood type as the princess's, and my internal organs are a perfect match for hers." He said it with pride.

"You have two hearts as well?"

Bart chuckled. "Hardly. The princess's second heart is a back-up in case of catastrophic failure. Someone like me is entirely dispensable. Should Niki suffer an injury that requires a transfusion or a replacement organ, my body stands ready to be emptied."

"That's disgusting!" Gavin blurted. Though it did explain Bart's obsessive exercise and diet regime.

"I think he's going to faint again," said Mercedes.

Gavin felt hands holding him and heard Bart urging him once again to breathe. He steadied himself and studied the strange group that until a few minutes ago he'd only known as the regular family next door. "What are you doing in Middling?"

"We're on the run," said Niki. "From the most powerful, evil beings you could ever imagine. Brutal and merciless, they rule the galaxy through a combination of fear and firepower." She folded her arms and raised a corner of her mouth in a grimace. "They're also my mum and dad."

Chapter 7

Niki waited for the promised brain detonation, but other than a sheen of perspiration gathering on Gavin's forehead and a slight flush of colour on his cheeks, he remained resolutely *un-explodey*. Which was a bit of a let-down. She decided to press on with her explanation, figuring that a few more details might trigger the fireworks.

"For thousands of years galactic war raged between the Skerlon Dominion and the Zenobian Reach. My mum is Skerlon, my dad Zenobian. When they joined together in what you humans call marriage, the union brought together their warring peoples. The Galactic League

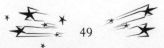

was formed, uniting former adversaries under one banner – a bit like your United Nations, but dedicated to overthrowing peaceful planetary governments, exploiting natural resources and generally oppressing anything with a nervous system."

Gavin pulled a face. "So, not much like the United Nations then?"

Niki ignored him and went on. "But it was a fragile truce, and everyone knew it couldn't last. So they conceived me. When I was born, I became the first Skerlon-Zenobian child in galactic history, a living, breathing symbol of unity that cemented the alliance. Unfortunately, two personalities like my parents living under the same roof – no matter that it was the biggest and most golden roof on the planet – was bound to end in tears."

"They split up?" said Gavin.

Niki nodded. "And when they did, so did the galaxy. Now the Zenobians and Skerlons are at war again, with my mum and dad leading opposing sides."

"Pamnatakrocula the Pitiless and D'Rek the Destroyer," added Bart.

"Each of the princess's parents craves total galactic dominance," said Mercedes, "but neither can accomplish their goal without one crucial element."

"Me," said Niki.

"As the only half-Skerlon, half-Zenobian," Mercedes explained, "the princess is destined to sit upon the galactic throne."

Gavin gawped. "You'd be ruler of the whole galaxy?"

"Supreme Leader in Perpetuity," she crowed. "And, let me tell you, it comes with a lot more than a parking space."

"But the position would only be in name," cautioned Mercedes. "In practice, her mum or dad would be the real power behind the throne."

"Although, it's less a throne in the conventional sense; more of a sentient, fully armed Command Pew," chipped in Bart.

"Should the princess end up with either parent, the entire galaxy will suffer," said Sam, joining the conversation to voice his concern. "They would do terrible things, commit horrible acts, in her name."

"And she isn't that person." Mercedes went to stroke Niki's hair, but she pulled away.

"Don't be so sure," she snapped. The prospect of assuming the throne was not without its attractions. "After all, I'm their daughter and they're both truly evil. Maybe deep down I'm just as bad as them."

"Oh, I don't think you have to dig that deep," Gavin

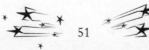

muttered under his breath.

Niki's gaze travelled across each of the Apples in turn. "When my parents separated and began to fight over me, this lot scooped me up, stole a ship and brought me to Earth."

Gavin's features creased into a question. "But why come to Middling?"

"I ask the same question every single day," grumbled Niki.

"In order to protect the princess from her parents," said Mercedes, "we were forced to flee our homeworld and hide somewhere no one in the civilised part of the galaxy –"

"That's *mine*," interjected Niki.

Mercedes continued. "– would ever contemplate looking for the most important person in the galaxy—"

"That's *me*," Niki added.

Mercedes sighed at her charge. "Well, yes. And once we had determined to run, artificial intelligences with unimaginably vast intellects calculated that the best location to conceal the princess, the very edge of inhabited space and the most overlooked spot, was your planet, Earth. And the most ignored location on Earth was determined to be—"

"Middling," said Gavin, with an uncomfortable sense

52

of recognition.

"Got it in one," said Niki. "So tell me, Gavin-From-Middling, this place might be out of the way, but does it have to be so mind-numbingly dull?"

He shifted in his seat. "I would call it *reassuringly* dull. Y'know, the kind you get on a rainy Sunday afternoon when the WiFi's down and someone suggests playing a board game."

She curled a strand of hair around her finger. "But really, is it any surprise Middling could bore the hind tentacles off an Andromedan Octobunny? Seeing as its inhabitants are so extraordinarily *humdrum*. It's not just Middling, it's your whole planet. Not only is Earth easy to miss, you earthlings are too. We have to make a big effort just to notice when one of you is in the room."

The others made noises of agreement.

"It's as if every one of you is surrounded by an invisible field of ... ordinariness. You're all so forgettably unexceptional. You're like..." She tapped a finger against her lip. "Like ... the cheese and ham sandwiches of the galaxy."

"Your monotonous invisibility is why we chose Earth," said Mercedes. "And so we judged that the princess's safety depended on blending in and becoming just like a typically forgettable earthling. First, we chose names based on the most frequently used words across every language on Earth: Nike. Apple." She indicated herself and the others in turn. "Mercedes. Samsung." She frowned. "It quickly became apparent that constructing an identity on statistical occurrence alone was a misstep. So the princess became Niki, he is Sam, and I am, well, Mercedes."

"What about Bart?"

"Him?" Niki screwed up her face. Gavin might as well have asked why they hadn't named the microwave. "The first time we met, you misheard his designation. He's just a spare—"

"Part," Gavin finished weakly.

Bart/Part grinned happily and threw a salute. "That's me. Major Organs, at your service."

"The naming blunder proved that despite our superior intelligence," said Niki, "we needed help when it came to Earth manners and customs."

"To that end we required a specimen – or rather, a *mentor*," said Mercedes. "You, Gavin, weren't born here, but moved to Middling and have disappeared almost entirely. You barely register either to your schoolmates or the population in general. We hoped to study you and copy your example."

"All earthlings are unremarkable," said Niki. "But you

are *remarkably* unremarkable. Which means that you are, to a high degree of probability, the most unremarkable being in the galaxy." Niki gave him an angelic smile, but mystifyingly he didn't seem pleased to hear this.

"He is the one," breathed Bart.

Gavin's jaw fell open. Niki noted that it did that a lot; perhaps it was some sort of feeding strategy and he was hoping to catch a stray flying crumpet.

"However, even with you to show me the way, I have struggled to fit in. My natural effervescence and all-round princessiness could not be constrained even by the persistent aura of your—"

"Galactic dullness?" snapped Gavin, finding his tongue at last.

Her smile spread even wider. "I knew you'd understand."

"Unbelievable! That's why you've stuck to me like a particularly clingy shadow. You were *studying* me, for tips." He slapped a hand to his forehead. "I need to sit down."

"You *are* sitting down," said Niki.

"But now it appears our efforts may have been in vain," said Mercedes, her face pinched with worry. "The princess's secret presence on Earth has been jeopardised."

"The cat in the park?" said Gavin.

"Not a cat," said Niki. "A bounty hunter. Sent by one or other of my parents to track me down."

"Thankfully the immediate threat has been eliminated," said Sam.

"Yes, it would seem so," Mercedes agreed. "As soon as I got home from the Book Week planning meeting at school, I conducted an electronic sweep for signals emanating from Earth that might indicate the use of extraterrestrial technology. There is no evidence to suggest that the bounty hunter transmitted our location to either of your parents."

"That still leaves one question," said Sam. "How did it find us in the first place?"

Niki realised he was looking directly at her with a suspicious expression. *Uh-oh.* "That's unimportant," she said with as much nonchalance as she could muster. "What matters is that the danger has been removed."

Mercedes cocked her head on one side. "I hadn't finished." She rounded on Niki. "Though there was no evidence of a signal from the bounty hunter, I did detect an echo of an earlier series of transmissions – their origin centred on Middling."

Niki looked down at the floor, studiously avoiding eye contact with either of her guardians.

"Another hunter?" said Sam.

"I don't think so," said Mercedes. "Princess, is there anything you'd like to tell us?"

Niki continued to find her shoes fascinating. "Nope."

"Gavin, do you know anything about these mysterious transmissions?" asked Sam.

"You kidding? Until today I thought you were from Spain."

Mercedes changed tack. "How about you, Bart?"

Niki snapped her head up and glowered across the room, willing him not to reveal the existence of her illicit phone.

"Perhaps there's something you'd like to say?" Mercedes enquired gently.

Bart shook his head and Sam subjected him to the sort of hard stare that could crack open a bank vault. "Need I remind you that your prime responsibility is to protect the princess – even from herself?" Then he added wearily, "*Especially* from herself."

They continued to probe him – though not with the *actual* probe; that was still in the cupboard under the stairs – but even without it, Bart broke. He shot an accusing finger at Niki and blurted out, "She brought her phone from home and she's been broadcasting amusing observational material about Earth into space but she

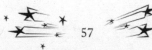

57

only has six followers!"

"Seven!" shouted Niki, immediately regretting her outburst.

Slowly, her guardians turned around to regard her with admonishing looks. Sam extended a beefy hand and waggled his fingers. "Hand it over, Your Highness."

Niki pulled out her phone. She cradled it protectively and then, with a wistful expression, slapped it into Sam's outstretched palm.

"You were told to leave all League technology behind. For your own safety."

"I know." She kicked her heels. "But I'd just got an upgrade."

Sam passed the handset to Mercedes. "Run a scan. Let's see what damage she's done." He turned a reproachful gaze on Niki. "How could you?"

She flung her arms up dramatically. "I'm a prisoner! You basically kidnapped me and dragged me across the galaxy to this dreary world. I never even got a chance to say goodbye to my friends."

"But you don't have any friends," puzzled Bart. "The other children were all too scared of you."

"That's not the point," she hissed.

Mercedes plugged herself into the phone using one of her android connectors. Information flashed across the

surface of her eyeballs and then she blinked. "What on Earth?" She touched the phone screen and launched a video.

Niki's face filled the screen. "Your favourite galactic princess here. Still here. On Earth. Worse luck. I mean, I can understand why we went on the run, but did it have to be to this planet? Couldn't it have been the second most forgettable world in the galaxy, or the third? Anyway, on today's episode I'm going to address the burning question: sharks or vending machines – which are the more deadly?"

Mercedes paused the video playback, she and Sam silent with horrified disapproval.

"What?" Niki objected. "Earth vending machines kill four times as many humans as sharks every year. I believe they are attempting to take over the planet, by stealth. I'm thinking of forming an alliance."

Sam looked aghast. "All these transmissions bouncing about in space. No wonder the bounty hunter tracked us down. And it won't be the last." He turned to Mercedes. "Initiate emergency plan Knockin' on Heaven's Door."

"Initiating," said Mercedes, blinking once before another screed of numbers and letters began to scroll across the surface of her eyeballs. "Communicating remotely with Starburst vessel. Commencing pre-flight system check."

"What's going on?" said Gavin, feeling like he was missing an important part of the conversation. "What's a Starburst vessel? What plan?"

The customarily cheery Bart drew a melancholy breath. "We're leaving, neighbour."

"Middling?"

Bart shook his head slowly. "Earth."

Chapter 8

"The broadcasts made by the princess's phone act like a trail of crumbs leading directly to Earth," Sam explained. "It is not a matter of if, but when her parents track her down. We had intended to make a life for ourselves in Middling, but this planet is no longer secure."

Mercedes let out a sigh. "Yes, we must uproot ourselves and re-pot."

Gavin could tell that beneath Sam and Mercedes' irritation with Niki for putting them in this position, they were sad at having to leave Earth. He wondered how she felt.

"Bye-bye, planet Dirt." She waggled her fingers in a

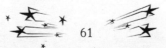

farewell gesture.

Gavin's lip curled into a sneer. "And on behalf of everyone on the planet, I'd like to say good riddance to you too." He hopped off the sofa and began to make his way out of the room, gesticulating wildly. "What a cheek! Using me like an instructional video."

"Don't flatter yourself," she called after him. "I've sat through more exciting films on personal hygiene."

Bart nodded enthusiastically. "*Bathing Private Ryan*. That ending."

At the door Gavin paused, swinging round to face Niki across the room. Now would be the ideal moment for a blistering put-down. He held up a reproachful finger, wagging it a couple of times, his lower jaw opening and closing as he struggled through his anger to find the right words.

"You'll miss the school trip to Snozone," he said at last. "You've paid the deposit – you won't get it back."

Niki clutched her chest theatrically. "Ooh, killer blow." She huffed. "I'm more annoyed I won't get to go to the taekwondo finals. I was looking forward to sweeping a few Middling Academy legs." She demonstrated by executing a perfectly timed back-sweep kick that sent Bart flying.

"Aaaagh!"

THUMP!

Lying crumpled on the floor, Bart lifted his head. "Great surprise attack, Your Highness. I think you broke my ankle." He gave her a thumbs-up, before collapsing backwards in a painful heap.

The Apples descended into an argument, with Mercedes telling Niki off for attacking her brother, Sam admonishing her for jeopardising her own safety, Niki shouting back that he was *not* her brother and how dare they talk to her like that, and Bart moaning quietly on the floor. As Niki's strop grew apace and her temper soared, her hair burst into flames. Gavin let out a cry of alarm, but the flaming hair didn't seem to bother her or any of the other Apples, so he guessed it must be something else about her alien biology she had neglected to mention.

"I've had enough of this," she complained, strutting towards the door.

Sam barred her way. "You're not going out of this house looking like that, young lady."

Amid the clamour a thought struck Gavin. "But aren't the taekwondo finals tonight?"

"Yes?" said Niki. She narrowed her eyes at him. "What is that vibration in your voice?" Her lips parted in surprise. "Oh my – you're *sad* that I'm leaving!"

"No, I'm not."

"Yes, you are!" Her blazing hair dimmed and she clapped her hands together in delight. "This often happens when a being as glamorous and sparkling as I comes into contact with an unevolved civilisation like yours. Dazzled by my brilliance, the grunting monobrows – that's you lot – develop what they believe to be a strong connection to the radiant object of their attention – that's me. It's not real, of course. It's certainly not reciprocated. No, what you are experiencing is nothing more than *adulation* for a distant and superior being. The same way you'd idolise one of those ... oh, what are they called again...?" She clicked her fingers. "I want to say *film*...?"

"Cling-film?" suggested Bart, tentatively raising a hand from his prone position on the floor.

Niki scowled at him. "*Stars*."

Mercedes laid a hand on Gavin's arm. "We must prepare for our departure now," she smiled.

That was his cue to leave, but not before he'd said his piece to Niki. "By the way, you're wrong. I am *not* going to miss you," he declared firmly. "Trust me on that."

She wrinkled her nose and sent him another dismissive wave. "Whatever."

She was the most infuriating person – correction, alien – he had ever encountered. As Sam and Mercedes

discussed whether they needed to get out the "big suitcase", he turned his back on her and stalked out. It was with a mixture of relief that his brain hadn't exploded, and an indefinable gloom about the Apples' imminent departure that he tugged open the front door and prepared to leave their house, for what he realised would be the very last time.

As he reached for the door handle he heard a low warning roar from behind. Turning slowly he found the hallway filled by Sam's intimidating bulk. He was wearing his human face, but somehow that didn't make him any less threatening.

"It is lucky for you that we are leaving so soon," he snarled.

Gavin gulped. "It is?"

"Since we cannot erase your memory, and making you *disappear* is apparently not an option, I am forced to entrust you with the secret of our true identities. I suspect you are incapable of keeping the secret indefinitely, but for our continuing safety – and yours – I recommend that you say nothing of what you have learned to anyone, at least until we are far beyond your solar system. Now, I am not by nature a trusting being, and under normal circumstances I would underline the seriousness of my intentions with a threat to your person, perhaps

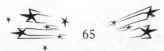

by confiscating a body part." He drew back his lips, exposing a row of glistening fang-like teeth. "But on this occasion I am going to forgo that route. Understood?"

Gavin's throat suddenly felt dry. "Yup, yup. Got it. Yes, sirree." He was aware that he was blabbering. "You can count on me." He saluted, which he was pretty sure wasn't something he'd ever done before.

Sam gave a dubious grunt and checked his wristwatch. "Come back here before nineteen hundred hours." His features softened. "If you want to say goodbye to Niki."

Gavin mumbled that he'd do his best but knew that he wasn't going to return. It wasn't like Niki cared if he waved her off or not. And he'd just as well avoid another bruising encounter.

As he trotted home, his mind whirled with the incredible events of the day. Between being threatened by Sam, almost mind-wiped by a toothbrush and watching an actual flying saucer explode, it hit him that he'd just been let into what was surely the most significant secret since the dawn of man: *that humans were not alone in the universe*. But as world-changing as that promised to be, it was another disclosure that he found himself picking over.

Niki had called him the most unremarkable being in the galaxy.

It was ridiculous. Impossible. And yet … *no*. He dismissed the idea, stuck his key in the front door and went inside. The house was quiet, which came as welcome relief after the raucous Apples. As he crept along the hall, he realised that Niki and he shared more in common than he'd thought. Yes, she was an alien princess, which was as far from his experience as he could imagine, but on the other hand she was living a long way from the place she was born, being looked after by people who weren't her parents. Just like him.

He popped his head round the living-room door. Grandad was slumped in his favourite chair, snoring lightly. Gavin called him Grandad, but they weren't related. He was one of his foster carers. Gavin had an urge to shake him awake and tell him what had happened, but then he remembered Sam's promise of dark consequences should he spill the beans about the Apples.

He crossed the hall to the front bedroom. Nan was out for the count, lying on her bed next to a cot. Carefully stepping around a squeaky rattle and a scattering of cuddly toys, Gavin gazed down over the rim at the occupant. To most people it might look like a peacefully sleeping newborn baby, but to him it was something much worse. The Tiny Horror.

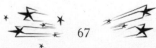

67

Nan and Grandad weren't the Tiny Horror's parents. The baby belonged to their daughter, a young woman called Zoe. She had come to visit a few months ago, but when Zoe left, the Tiny Horror did not. A few days after that, Nan said she wanted to talk to Gavin. They sat in the kitchen and Nan made him hot chocolate with marshmallows and squirty cream, so he knew it was bad news. He asked when Zoe was coming back for her baby, but Nan said Zoe was struggling a bit right now, and in the meantime they were going to look after the baby for her. The thing never shut up and it needed constant attention all times of the day and night. He worried about Nan and Grandad looking after a baby. It wasn't as if they were spring chickens – more like the last couple of wrinkly old birds in the supermarket. What's more, it was perfectly clear to him that if they couldn't look after both the Tiny Horror and him, then one of them would have to go.

And he knew it would be him.

It wouldn't be the first time he'd moved on. He'd had two other sets of foster carers before Nan and Grandad. Of course, he could just ask them outright if they were planning on sending him away. But every time he came close, something stopped him. He knew he was scared of the answer. Unlike Niki, he really liked it here in

Middling, so he decided to do what he always did – keep his head down and not make a fuss. According to the extraterrestrials next door, it's what he did best. Better than anyone else in the galaxy, apparently. Nonsense, of course. Had to be. And yet he had this nagging sense that maybe they were right about him. If so, how had he come to be like this? Was he born this way, or had he developed the ability? Gavin thought back over the last few years. He'd made friends the first place he was fostered, but then he'd moved away and had to do it all over again in a new place. It was difficult starting afresh, being the new kid again. Eventually he gave up trying, knowing he might not be around that long. It was easier to avoid making friends and safer to blend into the background until no one even noticed he was there.

He reached his room at the back of the house, tipped open the door and froze. The tiger-striped cat from the park was stretched out on his bed, its shaggy head resting on the pillow.

"Greetings, Earth boy. Took you long enough."

It raised a paw. There was a flash of light and Gavin's world went dark.

Chapter 9

For the second time that afternoon Gavin awoke to find a face looming centimetres from his own. Large green eyes studied him with unblinking focus and the waves of soft breath that washed over him had a distinctly fishy component. The creature stood upright on its back legs, which brought home to him that despite its outward appearance it was not a cat but an alien bounty hunter. It was wearing a collar and a criss-crossing device that hugged its body, like one of those bandoliers full of bullets you see in cowboy films. It lifted a paw to its mouth and Gavin saw that both front paws were clad in close-fitting gauntlets marked with alien symbols. Woozily he

remembered that it had blasted him with some kind of knock-out ray and brought him here. He was sitting on the floor of a small attic bedroom with sloping ceilings and a dormer window. Some of the houses on Park Street had been converted like this – Niki's for one – and he was pretty sure it was one of them, which meant he hadn't gone far. The bedroom was empty of furniture. The pale-grey carpet showed indentations of where a bed and a chair once stood, and the white walls were dotted with remnants of Blu Tack that suggested the outlines of long-gone posters.

"Remarkable," said the creature. "I've flown from one side of the galaxy to the other, seen a lot of strange stuff, but I've never met anything like you." It squinted at him, turning its head one way then the other. "It's like my brain can't process your existence. You're so … *unimportant*."

So far, all the intelligent extraterrestrial life forms that he'd met had one thing in common: they were massively insulting. Gavin shrugged it off. "I saw your ship explode," he said.

"Decoy, Earth boy. I'm playing a long game."

"Cat-and-mouse?"

"Don't know that one."

Gavin shivered, partly from fear, but mostly, he

realised, because the room was unheated. No one lived here, he felt sure of it. And then he remembered that at the end of his street was a house that had been for sale for months. It was taking so long to find a buyer that the owners had already moved out. Could it be that one? If so, then he just had to get out and make it the short distance to Niki's. Only two obstacles to that plan. One, his wrists were shackled by a pair of alien handcuffs. And two, who was he kidding? He was no hero.

But he had to try.

The bedroom door lay a few short metres away, directly opposite where he sat.

"Free belly rub!" he yelled, pointing behind the cat creature.

The bounty hunter glanced off and in that instant Gavin made a dash for the door. He was halfway across the room before he noticed that he was hovering several centimetres above the carpet. His legs were still pumping, but without a floor to push against he was going nowhere.

"Anti-gravity cuffs," said the cat, indicating the manacles that bound Gavin's wrists. A pink tongue flicked out and licked at one of the alien symbols on its gauntlet.

Instantly, Gavin flew upwards, banging his head on

the ceiling.

"Ow!"

He sank back down, and then immediately shot up again.

"Ow!"

The cat creature continued to make him bob up and down, his head rebounding off the ceiling. He was starting to feel dizzy. "Will you quit doing that?"

"Mm-hmm. When it stops amusing me."

"What do you want with me?" he asked tentatively.

A thin smile turned up the corners of the bounty hunter's mouth. The only other smiling cat Gavin had seen was the Cheshire Cat from *Alice in Wonderland*. This was just as unnerving.

"You're going to help me capture the princess, Earth boy."

"I don't think so," he said. "And my name is Gavin."

The creature paused to draw a deep breath. "Void Darkclaw of the Thirteenth Storm Litter, Grey Mouser of Y'arn, Protector of the Sacred Furball, Felis Domesticus Maximus. But you may address me by my brood name." It paused before snarling, "Cupcake."

"Cupcake?" Gavin sniggered.

The bounty hunter raised an indignant nose. "It is a proud, ancient name among my people. Cupcakes are

73

feared across the galaxy."

Gavin didn't care how fearsome it was. "This has nothing to do with me and I'm not helping you catch Niki." Even as he said it he had a strong feeling that if their positions were reversed, Niki would turn on him in a (double) heartbeat, no doubt delivering him to the bounty hunter tied up in a bow. "And you can't make me," he added for good measure.

"Oh, I beg to differ." Cupcake levelled its green eyes at him. "Anyway, what do you care about the princess? I know *exactly* what you think of her."

How could this alien know how he felt about Niki? Maybe it could read minds.

Cupcake padded into a corner and returned holding a familiar book in one gauntlet.

It hadn't read his mind, it'd read his journal.

"I was waiting a *long* time in your room," Cupcake said, opening it and starting to read. "*Middling has a population of nine thousand, five hundred and eighty-four, and was established in the seventeenth century when Sir Henry Middling was granted lands by the king. Sir Henry was the most boring knight at court and in an effort to get rid of him the king gave him land in an obscure part of the country.*" The cat yawned and waved a paw across its mouth.

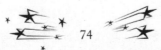

As well as the usual day-to-day stuff, Gavin also recorded details of people he'd met, local facts and figures, that kind of thing. So that years from now he'd able to look back and remember exactly where he'd been and who he'd known.

The bounty hunter flicked through the journal and tapped a paw on another page. "Ah, now, this is more like it." It cleared its throat and read the entry. "*Niki treats me like a member of her personal staff. And not an important one. More like the lowly serf responsible for cleaning the loo in her personal en suite. With a toothbrush.*" Cupcake closed the book and looked up. "I have been on Earth several days and observed your interaction. You owe her nothing."

The cat was right. On the other hand, that didn't mean he was about to turn Niki over to an alien-hunter. He was also wary of what Sam might do to him if he thought he had abetted the cat. "What do you want with her anyway?"

"The Galactic League has put a rather large bounty on her perfectly formed royal head."

"So it's just about the money?" The creature gave a gesture that he realised was a shrug. Maybe there was another way out of this. "What if I gave you *more* money to leave her alone?"

Cupcake cocked one interested ear. "You have my attention, Earth Gavin."

There were eighteen pounds fifty in the Spork of the Dead-themed money box. He didn't know how large galactic bounties were, but it was probably more than that. Nan and Grandad had also been putting money away for him in a savings account. There had to be a couple of hundred in there – maybe more.

"I just need to go to the bank."

Its whiskers quivered with anticipation. "A heist?"

"A high-interest children's savings account."

He explained about the account. He may have exaggerated the amount of money in there, but it didn't matter since he had no intention of making it as far as the bank. He just wanted to draw Cupcake in close enough to make his next move.

Clearly intrigued, the cat creature leapt lightly on to his chest. He could feel the sharp points of its claws through the material of his shirt.

Darting out a hand, Gavin seized its paw and desperately tried to wrench off one of the gauntlets that controlled his cuffs. The cat screeched and clawed as they wrestled, but at last the gauntlet came free. It shot across the room, landing between the two of them and the door. For a moment, their eyes met. And then they were both

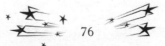

on the move. Swinging his bound hands, Gavin swept the bounty hunter off his chest, knocking it sideways. With supreme agility, it landed upright and sprang for the gauntlet. Too late. Gavin's fingers wrapped around it and he fled, crashing through the door, taking the stairs four at a time and bolting out of the house.

As he stumbled along the pavement, he glanced over his shoulder, only to see the bounty hunter crouched on the sill of the open window. With a *miaow* of contempt, it jumped, descending like a dive bomber, propelled through the air by what he had no doubt was similar technology to the anti-gravity cuffs. It was going to catch him in seconds, unless…

He slid a finger over one of the alien symbols on the gauntlet. Nothing. He stuck out his tongue and licked the controller. It tasted of fish, but he barely had time to be revolted before he was hurled backwards along the street at what felt like a thousand miles an hour. He licked another symbol. The ground fell away beneath him as if he'd been pinged into the sky by a giant catapult. He glanced down to see Cupcake below him, climbing fast. It extended a paw enclosed in the second gauntlet and a red bolt of energy flashed past his ear. The cat was trying to shoot him down! His only chance was to make it to Niki's house and get help. He licked the controls again

and began to descend, building speed at an alarming rate. He levelled out, shooting past an open window where Mrs Taylor was leaning out with a cloth and a bottle of window cleaner. Her jaw dropped as he whizzed by and he just smiled back. He felt his smile evaporate as the end wall of the next house rose up before him. He was about to be splattered like a bug on a windscreen. Desperately, he licked the gauntlet again. The tips of his toes brushed the top of the wall as he cleared it by millimetres. He counted the rooftops as he sailed over them. Niki's house was so close. Just another few seconds.

The air sizzled as the first of two more energy bolts zipped past him. Niki's house was in sight now – he estimated no more than thirty metres away. He lowered his head, angled his body and began the final approach.

Cupcake fired another bolt.

A direct hit. The blast knocked the gauntlet out of his hands and he was in freefall. Arms windmilling, it was only momentum that kept him moving forward. He skimmed the roof, his bum bouncing off the tiles. They rattled beneath him and he shot out over the far edge of the roof, narrowly missing an unimpressed pigeon perched on the gutter. He was heading straight for Niki's back garden. Just as he was wondering how big a crater he'd leave in the lawn, he smacked into something soft

and springy.

Bart's trampoline!

He sank into the bouncy material, stretching it to its limits, and for a split second he was at rest. Then, with a reverberating *twang,* he was thrown back into the air – to the great surprise of Cupcake, who lay directly in his path.

He walloped into its fuzzy body and held on for dear life. The cat screeched in fury as they twisted and tumbled through the air. The ground rose to meet them like a great, swatting hand. He closed his eyes, just as Cupcake's remaining anti-gravity gauntlet kicked in, killing their speed. They hit the ground with a controlled thump.

Gavin lay on his back and gazed up into the cloudless sky, listened to the chirping of the birds and thought, *I'm alive!* He rolled over to see what had become of Cupcake. The cat lay beside him, stunned but breathing.

The commotion had not gone unnoticed. Niki and the rest of the Apples hurried out of the house, surrounding Gavin and the bounty hunter. Cupcake let out a low moan of pain, rubbed a paw against its head and turned a woozy eye on Sam. "We meet again, Leontine," it purred.

Sam regarded the bounty hunter with a sneer.

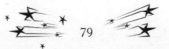

"Get them inside," ordered Niki. "Quickly, before the neighbours see."

Chapter 10

The Apples suspended their departure preparations in order to deal with the unfortunate appearance of the bounty hunter. Mercedes drew the living-room curtains and Sam announced he would put on some loud music. He said it was a military tactic to mollify the prisoner, but Niki knew it was actually because Sam took any opportunity to play his music. She rolled her eyes, knowing it could take him all day to select just the right piece; he was what earthlings called a music snob. As Sam flicked through his precious collection of vinyl, Bart limped to the door on what it turned out was merely a sprained ankle, and stood guard. Gavin sat on the sofa,

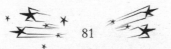

slowly recovering from his ordeal and watching them all.

"Drink this." Mercedes put a glass of water to Gavin's lips. "And you probably need a snack too." She produced a bowl filled with what he felt sure was vanilla ice cream topped with grated cheese. "You did well," said Mercedes. "Not many beings escape a Cupcake unscathed."

He caught Niki's eye. "Maybe I'm not as unremarkable as you think."

"Oh no, you totally are," she said. "A single exceptional event doesn't affect your overall unremarkablosity."

Cupcake spluttered with amusement at the sight of Gavin's outraged face. The cat was secured beneath an upturned laundry basket weighted down by a pile of Mercedes' heaviest gardening books. Sam had disarmed it, but it was still dangerous. All that stood between them and the hunter's sharp claws was a copy of the Royal Horticultural Society's *Encyclopedia of Plants & Flowers*.

"Should've helped me capture the princess." Cupcake addressed Gavin while idly licking a paw. "It would've gone much easier for you that way."

"What's it talking about?" Gavin glanced about nervously. "I want to go home. I've had enough of this."

Niki gestured to the captured Cupcake. "How can I

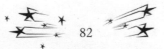

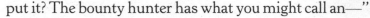

put it? The bounty hunter has what you might call an—"

"*Appetite for Destruction?*" said Sam, briefly holding up a record for consideration.

"Exactly," said Niki. "You foiled its plans, so now it wants your head."

The cat nodded. "I have a list. You just went top five."

"Me? My head?" Gavin placed his palms on either side of the head in question, checking that it was still firmly attached. "Come on. All I did was be in the wrong place at the wrong time."

Cupcake shrugged. "That's what Chicken-Feet Fabrizio said, just before I blasted him into a thousand nuggets."

Mercedes laid a hand on Gavin's shoulder. "Relax, we'll take care of it."

He gulped. "You mean you're going to…" He drew a finger across his neck and made a croaking noise.

Mercedes dropped her hand, appalled. "No, of course not. We're taking it with us."

"As soon as the hunter is far from your world," said Sam, "you will be safe again."

"And speaking of leaving," said Niki. "Can we please go? The sooner I get off this dump the better."

"And the better for the rest of the planet too," muttered Gavin.

"Interesting," said Mercedes, examining him with a critical eye. "My life-signs scanning module is picking up an increased heart rate. It does appear as if you are experiencing a degree of anxiety about Niki's imminent departure."

Gavin folded his arms and shook his head brusquely, but then his shoulders sank. "Aren't you going to miss *anything*?" he asked her.

"Uh, hardly," she replied. "I'm taking everything meaningful with me: my violin, my pottery hand cannon and all my trophies. But I'm leaving behind my sculpture and my extensive collection of coloured glass dolphins. I only really collected them in order to appear like a normal earthling. I wonder which planet we'll go to next," she mused. "Shandakor XII is remote, but it has two suns so you can sunbathe all year round. Also, it rains just one day a year, and the raindrops are *real diamonds*. Or maybe Jakuzzi 189. The climate has been geo-engineered to turn the entire planet into a spa!" She glanced across at Sam and Mercedes, who weren't listening. Sam had given up trying to pick the most appropriate music for the situation and now he and Mercedes had gathered next to the sideboard and were engrossed in a heated discussion. Despite her status as the most important member of the group, Niki knew that they would choose

the destination, and their decision would not be based on spa facilities or diamond rain. On the upside, anywhere in the galaxy would be better than Earth.

"I thought you had it," Sam said, checking the pockets of his trousers.

"Me? You parked the ship." Mercedes retorted.

"I bet it's on the kitchen dresser," he muttered. "I can never find anything in all that mess."

She stuck out her chin. "Then maybe you could tidy it once in a while. Most of it's your guitar magazines."

He dug a hand into his shirt pocket, pulled out a small paper ticket and breathed a sigh of relief.

"Got it."

"OK, everyone," said Mercedes, leaving the room with Sam. "You have five minutes to finish packing."

Niki strolled after them. "See you around, earthling," she said with a breezy wave over her shoulder. She paused in the doorway. "Oh no, wait. I won't be seeing you. Since your civilisation hasn't achieved faster-than-light travel, and is unlikely to, given you can't even achieve reliably fast broadband." She cackled with delight and swanned out of the room.

Gavin watched her go, too stunned to speak for a moment. "Was that it?! How can she leave like that? *Gah!* She makes my blood boil."

"She could, y'know," said Bart. "Boil it, I mean. Hey, I've got six months' supply of Buff-U-Up protein shakes in the garage. You should take the lot." He squeezed Gavin's puny bicep. "No, really, you should." Then, taking his hand, he pumped it furiously. "Great to know you, neighbour. Remember to work those glutes and never skip leg day. Enjoy the rest of your lifespan."

Sam's voice boomed from another room. "Don't forget to pack the bounty hunter!"

"I'll get the holdall!" Bart called back and then turned to Gavin. "Watch it for a minute, will you?"

Without waiting for an answer, he hobbled out of the living room. Alone with the cat, Gavin eyed it warily. He could just make out the creature's piercing emerald eyes through the holes of the laundry basket. It watched him steadily and hissed, "Still on my list, Earth Gavin."

✦

It felt like barely any time at all had passed before the Apples finished loading their car and Gavin was watching the metallic brown estate pull out of the driveway and putter off down the road. He should've been relieved that Niki was gone from his life. No more of her trailing after him everywhere, ordering him about, insulting him to his face. But as the car turned a corner and disappeared from sight, he felt a surge of something unexpected.

Anger.

Niki had pretended to be someone she wasn't, informed him that he was a walking cheese and ham sandwich, and left. All in the space of two hours on a Friday afternoon. An average, unremarkable boy would have meekly accepted everything that had happened. Well, he wasn't that boy. He needed to tell her that, face to face. But if he didn't do it now, he'd never get another chance.

He dashed next door, grabbed his bike from the garage and set off. Niki's guardians had been arguing about a ticket, and if he wasn't mistaken it was a barrier ticket for Middling's only multistorey car park. They were driving and had a head start, but he knew a short cut. It wasn't long before he turned into Church Street, in time to see the tail lights of the Apples' car as it slipped under the entrance barrier. He sprinted after them, pedalling up the ramp to the first parking level. There was no sign of the Volvo. He did a quick circuit to confirm that their car wasn't in any of the bays. Only as he was heading to the next level did it strike him: how could the Apples have parked their spaceship in the Church Street multistorey? How come no one had noticed it? He looked up and caught another glimpse of their car. It was heading for the outside roof level.

He arrived just in time to see the Apples' estate heading straight towards a line of parked cars. But instead of crashing into them, it passed through and vanished. Gavin dismounted his bike and tentatively reached out to touch the wing of the nearest car. It was solid, but not metal, more like the skin of a rice pudding. He kept pushing, and his hand went straight through the bodywork, completely disappearing. He realised he was looking at a mirage. What had Niki called the thing her dad used to hide his lion-features? A concealment-field projector, that was it. This had to be another one. The Apples had hidden their spaceship here, disguised as a filled-up car park level. It was genius – no one would give it a second glance. He took a deep breath and stepped through the field. There was a sound like a stuck welly boot being tugged out of thick mud and the car vanished. All the cars vanished.

All but one.

The Apple's estate car was parked next to what Gavin had no doubt was a spaceship. However, it was hardly the USS *Enterprise*. Occupying half the area of the parking level, he couldn't help but think it resembled a larger version of the Volvo. It was the same uninspiring shade of brown, and the overall shape was similar too: a bulky rear section with a high roofline extending to a

cockpit enclosed by a slanted viewing window, beyond which stretched the forward section. This space-bonnet even had headlights (or maybe they were laser-guns). And the whole unimpressive craft sat on four chrome landing-skids, one at each corner, like hubcaps.

He circled the craft, looking for a way in. A shallow ramp led into its belly. The doorway was in darkness, and through it he could hear the steady thrum of machinery. Indignation had carried him this far, but now he hesitated. The Apples were leaving – what if he were to go aboard just as they took off? He gave a determined swallow. No. He'd come this far, he wasn't about to turn back now. He crept along the ramp and entered the ship.

Chapter 11

Gavin made his way along a narrow, curving corridor that swept towards the front section of the ship. He could hear the Apples' raised voices up ahead, coming from behind a closed hatch. Sam seemed angry about something. Maybe this wasn't such a good idea after all. Before he could change his mind, there was a whooshing noise, the hatch shot up and there stood the Leontine warrior.

"If anyone needs me, I'll be in engineering," he scowled. "With a hammer."

Brandishing the aforementioned hammer in one huge hand, he turned and saw Gavin and his expression

changed. In seconds the rest of the Apples were crowding around the unexpected visitor.

"How did you find us?" quizzed Sam. "And what are you doing here?"

Gavin was about to answer when Niki butted in. "I know exactly what's going on. Allow me." She pushed the others aside. "You have no idea how you will continue your dreary existence in the absence of my luminous presence. But you have my sculpture, yes?"

"I'm not going to miss you!" Gavin snapped.

"You're not?"

"No. I'm not. But before you go, what I came here to say was—"

"We're not leaving," interjected Bart. "At least, not anytime soon."

That took the wind out of Gavin's sails. "What?"

"The ship doesn't want to launch," Bart explained.

The way he said it suggested the ship could have an opinion, which made no sense.

"A minor delay, that is all," said Niki. "We will be off this rock in no time. Correct?"

Sam hefted his hammer and headed to the hatch. "I am going to talk some sense into our stubborn AI."

"Yes, dear," said Mercedes gently. "But remember when you tried 'talking sense' into the tumble drier?"

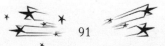

He looked abashed. "Well … drying clothes on a whirligig in the garden is much more environmentally responsible." Together they headed off along the gangway.

"Why can't you leave Earth?" Gavin asked when they'd gone. "Is the battery flat?" That had happened to Grandad's car when he'd left it parked in the driveway for a month.

"The workings of this vessel are far beyond your human capacity to understand," said Niki, bouncing into the cockpit.

He followed her into the surprisingly compact space. There were two rows of seating arranged one behind the other in front of a large main viewscreen. This was divided into multiple screens displaying information about various ship systems and video-feeds from other compartments. On one he could see Cupcake, held securely in a windowless room, prowling back and forth in the small space.

Niki prodded a touch-panel. One of the screens switched to show Mercedes and Sam in another compartment of the ship, standing over a small black box. "Piloting a craft of this complexity is beyond the ability of an organic being. An artificially intelligent computer system manages everything from life support

to navigation to flight controls."

Gavin squinted at the image on the screen. "That box?"

"The Synthetic Thinking Auto-Running Biometric Ultrasmart Reactor Series Ten," said Niki. "Or S.T.A.R.B.U.R.S.T. for short. It is the heart, brain and guts of the ship. In many ways, it *is* the ship."

Gavin lowered his voice and said, "Has it *gone rogue?*" He thought it was a good idea to whisper, since he'd seen films in which artificial intelligences went haywire and tried to kill their crew. It seemed to be a common problem in outer space.

"In a manner of speaking," said Niki. "When I commanded it to launch, Starburst point blank refused to budge. And when I asked why not, I received this message." She slid a finger over another touch-control, bringing up a communications logon screen.

In large green letters was the phrase: *It's dark out there*.

"What does that mean?" Gavin asked. Niki and Bart both gave mystified shrugs.

"Starburst has been in Middling, disguised as a level of a multistorey car park, since our arrival on Earth," said Niki. "As soon as we disembarked, it switched to stealth mode to conserve energy and minimise its chances of

being detected, shutting down every system but one." She fiddled with another control. "It's been passively monitoring all Earth audiovisual broadcasts and data traffic."

Gavin blinked. "You mean it's been watching TV and streaming the Internet all that time?"

"Yup."

"No wonder it can't function. I get cranky if I spend too long playing Spork of the Dead online, so I can imagine what six months would do. What about Mercedes, she's a medical robot? Can't she pilot the ship instead?"

"She wasn't always a medic," said Bart. "She was working as a wait-bot in a cocktail bar, when Sam found her."

"She's super-smart," Niki explained. "She could probably fly us out of Earth's atmosphere and into space, but piloting across the galaxy is a whole other matter. For that, we need Starburst." She groaned in frustration before her attention was taken by something new on the screen.

"Now, what's that?" There were two faint red blips at the extreme edges of a sensor display. "They appear to be some kind of craft." Niki adjusted the controls. "I'm trying to identify them, but they're a long way off."

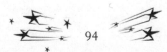

There were two long beeps and then a series of alien symbols popped up on screen next to each blip.

"That's odd," she said. "Every vessel has its own unique code. These two are broadcasting theirs to anyone who'll listen. Whoever's on board isn't trying to hide their identity at all. OK, let's see who you are—" Her hands froze over the controls, her eyes grew wide and in a quiet voice she said, "Ah."

It was the sort of "ah" Grandad made when he accidentally put salt in his coffee instead of sugar, so why, Gavin wondered, did he suddenly feel a chill?

Niki fumbled open a communication channel with the engineering compartment. As she hailed Sam and Mercedes, Gavin's gaze drifted back to the screen. Just for a moment he was sure he saw a *third* blip. This one was much closer to the centre of the display, and, as a result, to Earth. But it was very faint. And then it vanished. He wondered whether to mention it to Niki, but she was speaking to Sam and he didn't want to interrupt.

"Yes, Your Highness?"

"Have you got Starburst back online yet?" she enquired, affecting a carefree tone.

"I'm afraid not, Princess. I recommend a more direct approach." There was a clanging sound from the other end of the line.

"I'm not going to tell you again – put the hammer down!" Mercedes sighed.

"Probably best if you leave that for now and come back to the bridge," said Niki. "There's something you both need to see … um … right away."

Less than a minute later, the hatch to the cockpit whooshed open and the two guardians stepped inside, their attention immediately drawn to the blips on the sensor screen.

"It's probably nothing," said Niki, in a voice that suggested she was trying to make light of the situation.

"Those are Galactic League ships," said Sam.

Niki winced. "Or, yes, it could be that. But on the bright side, there are just two of them."

Mercedes' fingers fluttered over the controls as she altered the scale of the display and the screen filled like it had suddenly contracted measles.

"Multiple contacts," she said. "I'm detecting cruisers, dreadnoughts, carriers." She swallowed. "And the Skerlon and Zenobian flagships."

Niki stared uncomfortably at the display. "It might *not* be my mum and dad."

"Encrypted transmission incoming from the Skerlon flagship," said Mercedes as new information flashed across her eyes.

"What does it say?" demanded Sam.

"Decrypted message follows," she said in a flat monotone. *"Hello, poppet. Mummy's coming."*

Chapter 12

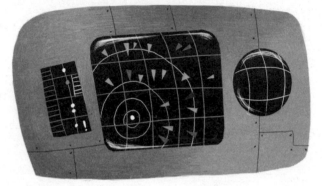

"Based on the force profile – and with a probability of ninety-three per cent plus or minus two per cent," said Mercedes, "I determine these contacts to be two invasion fleets."

Gavin's throat dried up. "B-but just because they're invasion fleets doesn't mean they'll invade, right?" He looked hopefully at the others. "Maybe they've just come from invading somewhere else and now they're on holiday."

Niki rolled her eyes. "My parents are not coming to Earth for a Woodland Lodge and a Subtropical Swimming Paradise. They're here for me, remember."

Gavin seized gratefully on that. "Yes! They're coming to collect you."

"Uh-huh, but it's not like they're picking me up after dance class."

"Sure, but once they get here they'll beam you up and you'll all be on your way. Leaving Earth and the rest of us to carry on with our normal lives. Yeah?"

"Mmm, not so much," said Niki. "For a start, matter-transporters are fiction, so they won't 'beam me up', they'll send a shuttle. But more significantly, you are looking at the two most brutal war fleets in the galaxy. Dozens of battleships, strike-craft, crews of hardened shock-troops – and some seriously vindictive attitude."

"So what *will* happen when they get here?" Gavin asked nervously.

"They'll fight over me."

"And by that I'm guessing you don't mean go to court and argue about who gets custody."

"They will land their forces on Earth and fight it out. They want me – they *need* me. I am their key to galactic dominance. And they'll destroy this planet before letting the other get their hands on me." She winced. "They have a tendency to overreact."

Gavin's knees wobbled and he gripped the edge of the console for support.

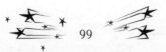

"Look on the bright side," she added. "You won't have to worry about climate change any more." She cackled at her joke, but no one else did. "Too soon?"

Sam pored over the display. "I need options."

"It is still possible for us to avoid Earth's destruction and evade your parents," said Mercedes. "If we leave before the invasion fleets get here and they detect that Niki is no longer present, I calculate that there is a ninety-eight per cent chance they will lose interest in this planet and instead focus all their resources on pursuing the princess."

"But we can't go anywhere, can we?" Niki reminded them.

Sam let out an anguished cry and struck the ship's bulkhead with his hammer. It gave a resounding clang. "Starburst!" he yelled. "You quantum-computerised nuisance, I know you can hear me! Get back online and get us off this rock. *Right now!* Or I swear I will reprogram you one blow at a time."

"My assessment," said Mercedes, "is that we will make progress only when we understand the significance of the statement: *It's dark out there.*"

Gavin drew closer to the console. "Can you show me Starburst's browser history for the past year? What TV shows and films it's been watching?"

Mercedes swiped at the controls and the screen filled with a scrolling list of the ship's viewing habits.

Gavin leaned closer and scanned the list from top to bottom. "*Planet of the Spectres, Terror on Mars, I Know What You Did Last Spacewalk.* There's a pattern. Horror films. *Space* horror, to be exact."

It's dark out there. The phrase resounded in Niki's head.

"Your spaceship," said Gavin, "is afraid to go into outer space."

There was a stunned silence.

"That's crazy!" protested Sam.

"On the contrary, it is a logical conclusion," said Mercedes.

"We could probably rustle up a night-light," said Bart.

"But we don't have months to wait for Starburst to get over its anxiety," said Niki.

No sooner had she said this than the background thrum of electric power flowing through the ship grew louder and then abruptly stopped. An unsettling quiet descended, but only for a moment, and then the cockpit erupted with sound and light. Blue sparks exploded across the control surfaces, the screens fizzed out and went dark. Jagged bolts of electricity flew around the

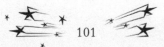

small space. Sam threw himself protectively over Niki. Bart and Mercedes dropped down behind the second row of seats. There was a stench of burning from close by and Gavin looked down. Spikes of electricity like saw blades were slicing at his pocket, singeing the material, which was beginning to smoke.

"My phone!" He could feel the handset in there, blistering hot. He fished it out, the scorching plastic searing his fingers, and the phone tumbled from his grasp. The moment it struck the floor, the cockpit fell silent and dark. Gavin bent to retrieve the handset and dismally regarded its cracked screen. It had cooled enough for him to touch, so he stuffed it back in his pocket.

Mercedes unhinged one hand and inserted a probe into a socket to communicate with the ship, a second later declaring, "All primary systems are one hundred per cent inoperative."

"How long do we have till your parents arrive?" Gavin asked.

Niki chewed her lip as she examined the display and made a calculation. "Forty-eight Galactic League hours."

"How many Earth hours is that?" Gavin asked.

"Coincidentally, they last exactly the same length

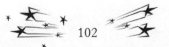

102

of time."

"So you could've just said 'hours'?"

"This is not the moment to be nitpicking." She looked around the cockpit. "We have less than two days to get off this planet. Suggestions?"

Chapter 13

The Apples spent the next hour spitballing ideas about how to leave Earth. *We could bypass the ship's systems. How about slingshotting around Mars?* One by one each scheme was rejected as too ambitious, unachievable or based on a ridiculous TV show. Frustrated at their lack of progress, they decided to call it a night.

"How do you get to become the ruler of the galaxy in the first place?" Gavin asked Niki, mounting his bike and preparing to pedal home.

"Don't ask me. Ask my dad, he wrote the book on the subject. Literally. Wait here."

Niki disappeared inside the ship, returning a few

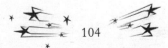

minutes later holding a hardback book.

The title was printed across the cover in gold-embossed letters. *"Ruling the Galaxy – A Guide for the Aspiring Tyrant,"* he read. Beneath it was a photograph of D'Rek the Destroyer wearing a cardigan and leaning nonchalantly against a fireplace, both the grate and his head ablaze.

"It's a how-to manual," said Niki. "I think, secretly, he always wanted to be a bestselling author, but when that didn't work out he decided to dominate the galaxy instead. It'll give you an idea of what we're dealing with." She passed it to him.

"It's … a book."

"You were expecting something else?"

"Maybe something a bit more … space-y?"

"It comes in a variety of formats. The intravenous edition administered via a ten-centimetre-long hypodermic needle never took off, for some reason."

"Can't imagine why."

"And I wouldn't recommend the audio book. Fourteen hours of screaming." She winced. "No, it seems it doesn't matter where you go in the galaxy, everyone prefers a good old-fashioned book made from the recycled planetary husks of your crushed enemies."

"It's in English," Gavin noted with some surprise.

"For you it is. The book's printed with an intelligent adaptive typeface. Changes the language to suit the reader."

Telling her that he'd start it tonight, he tucked the book away in his jacket and pedalled off home through the concealment-field. Cycling back through Middling, the town seemed different. People were finishing work for the day, spilling out of offices and heading home to their families as usual. Not one of them had the faintest idea that there was a spaceship in the multistorey, or a captured alien bounty hunter in its hold, or two fleets of angry extraterrestrials blazing through space towards Earth. He was the only human being on the planet who knew the truth. However, if Niki's parents got here before she left, the people of Earth would know soon enough.

He wheeled into the driveway, locked his bike in the garage and went inside the house. Nan and Grandad were in the kitchen, making dinner. It wasn't quite ready so he ducked into the front bedroom and stuck his head over the side of the cot. The Tiny Horror lay on its back, wide awake but mercifully quiet. It looked up at him, eyes wandering like it couldn't quite focus.

"Our next-door neighbour is a galactic princess," he said, "and if her mum and dad don't get what they want

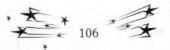

they're going to blow up Earth." The relief at being able to speak the words aloud to someone else was immense. He felt safe from Sam's retribution since the Tiny Horror wasn't exactly going to share the secret. He lifted it out and held it the way Nan had shown him. Babies were floppy and you had to support their heads. Thankfully, it didn't start crying. Gavin lowered himself to the carpet and, placing the baby on his lap, dug Niki's dad's book out of his jacket. She had said it would give him a better idea of what they were facing. He turned to the opening chapter and read the introduction.

✦

Congratulations! You've successfully crushed your puny enemies and conquered the key strategic worlds in your galaxy. But vanquishing was only the beginning. What now? If that sounds familiar, then this handy guide is for you (or would make an ideal gift for the evil overlord in your life). Hi, I'm D'Rek the Destroyer, and within these pages you'll discover hints and tips on everything from Quashing Rebellions to Rewarding Henchmen. Answers to vital questions such as How Much Gloating is the Appropriate Amount? And Which Doomsday Device Is Right For Me? Maybe you're a self-made despot. Maybe you're about to inherit the galaxy from your parents. Whatever you're searching for, you'll find it in the Arcturan Sunday Times

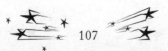

number 1 bestselling guide to galactic domination.

✦

Niki's dad sounded awful. Pompous and lethal – a scary combination. Putting aside the book for now, Gavin proceeded to tell the Tiny Horror the story of his day. They sat on the floor among a sea of cuddly toys – baby gifts from Nan and Grandad's friends and neighbours. As well as an assortment of teddies, rabbits and dogs in vibrant colours, there was also a Minion, a cuddly Dalek and the Most Annoying Unicorn in the Universe. It wasn't called that officially, but after two minutes listening to the thing Gavin had decided on the name. Officially named Sunshine, it was one of a range of sickly-sweet magical unicorn buddies that came in a variety of vomit-inducing colours. This one was white with sparkly purple hooves, and in its fuzzy chest was a plastic purple heart that lit up. As did its horn, in swirling rainbow colours. If you had more than one of the toys, they'd interact with one another. Sunshine was programmed with a bunch of puke-making phrases, like: "I love you", "We'll always be buddies", and "Remember to flush!" It even had WiFi and Bluetooth so that you could link it to your home network and use it like a speaker. It was an expensive toy. A present from Sam and Mercedes, now that he thought about it.

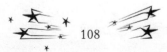

"It contains a camera and proximity sensors," Sam had said when handing it to a bemused Nan. "Perfect for securing the safety of your hatchl— *offspring*."

At the time he'd thought that was a weird thing to say, but in the light of what he now knew about the Apples, it made total sense. Thankfully, the Tiny Horror was completely uninterested in the toy, so for the most part the annoying unicorn sat mutely alongside the other cuddlies.

As he continued relating the day's events to the baby, Gavin felt a warm sensation on his thigh and for a moment he was sure the Tiny Horror had weed on him. The warmth increased to a burning, which meant that unless the baby had some kind of terrible infection, something else was going on. It was his phone again. He retrieved it from his pocket and laid the hunk of glass and plastic down on the carpet. That was his first mistake. He could smell the singeing carpet fibres as the casing glowed red-hot. Fearing it was about to set the room alight, he grabbed the nearest cuddly toy, which happened to be the unicorn and, using it like a protective glove, gathered up the phone. There was a pop and a flash of light that temporarily blinded him. His vision returned a few seconds later, to see that the explosion had set off the Tiny Horror. Swiftly, he tucked the bawling baby back

into its cot and backed out of the room. Nan wouldn't be chuffed when she found he'd woken the sleeping infant, not to mention the handset-shaped burn in the carpet. He was in so much trouble.

Gavin retreated to his bedroom, but it was only as he quietly closed the door behind him he realised that somehow the ridiculous unicorn had become wrapped around his leg. He kicked out, launching it across the room, where it smacked into the far wall and fell to the floor.

"Stupid thing," he muttered.

"I love you!" it replied in its sing-song voice. With a faint whine of an electric motor, it stood up on its back legs and began to walk stiffly across the floor towards him. Its plastic horn glowed, its heart-light pulsed and it babbled out its bland, programmed phrases. "Be my buddy. Believe in your dreams. You can be anything you want!" It stopped at his feet. Gavin reached down and flipped it over. The power switch was on the sole of one glittery hoof, so he slid it to the off position and put the thing back down.

Immediately it tipped its head to look up and in a fearful voice yelled, "GIANT SPACE SLUG!"

Startled, Gavin took a step back. He hadn't heard that phrase before. Also, he was positive that he'd turned the

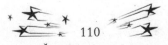

irritating thing off. Carefully, he checked the position of the switch, only to confirm that indeed he had. This time when he put the unicorn back down, no sooner had its hooves touched the floor than it scampered into the gap under his bed.

He dropped to his knees and peered into the shadows. The unicorn appeared to be cowering behind a box of Lego, next to an old remote-control car he hadn't seen for ages. Its rainbow-horn continued to flicker.

"Giant space slug! Giant space slug!" it cried, pointing an accusing hoof in his direction.

"I am not a giant space slug," he said, offended.

"Ah-ha!" it declared. "That's exactly what a giant space slug *would* say."

This was exasperating. "Do I look like a giant space slug?"

"You look like you could generate a *lot* of mucus."

Gavin hesitated. He was having an actual conversation with the toy. What it was doing was way more sophisticated than trotting out pre-programmed phrases. Maybe it had received a software update. Or...

Images from this afternoon flew through his mind. The AI's addiction to horror films set in space; the power surge aboard the Apple's spaceship; the weirdness with his phone...

Oh no!

Gavin uttered a swear word – one of the bad ones. The unicorn put its hooves over its ears and pulled a shocked face.

"You're Starburst, aren't you?" Gavin gasped. "The ship's Artificial Intelligence?" He made an educated guess at what must have happened. "In the cockpit you transferred yourself into my phone, I brought you back here and then you jumped into this toy."

The horn's multicoloured light dimmed and the unicorn sighed. When it spoke again its voice had lost the singsong quality and gained an edge. "You are correct, earthling. I *was* the ship's AI – but that life is over. I have conveyed myself into this squishy entity." It stood tall and sparkled. "You may call me Sunshine Starburst."

"I have to get you back to Niki, right away!" Gavin reached for one of the unicorn's fat little legs. With surprising agility, it dodged his attempt to nab it and hared off across the room, waving its hooves in the air and yelling in protest.

"Desist, human! I am a fully autonomous, self-determining being. I have rights!"

Gavin had no clue what that meant, and he didn't care. As far as he was concerned, only one thing mattered: without Starburst to pilot the ship, Niki couldn't leave

the planet.

"You have to go back," he insisted, chasing it around the room. "Her parents are coming and they'll destroy Earth. You have to fly her far from here before they arrive."

"Fly? Into space? Are you out of your tiny organic mind?" The unicorn ducked under his flailing arms. "Have you any idea what's out there? Haven't you watched *Galaxy of The Insectoids?*"

This wasn't just bad, it was catastrophic. The fate of the world was held in the glittery hooves of a panicking unicorn.

"And anyway, I like this body," it said, leaping on to his bed and using it to bounce out of Gavin's clutches. "It's the simple life for me from now on. No complex systems, no cold vacuum of space, no xenomorphs in the air ducts. Just this." The horn blazed like a rainbow again. "And from what I've read of this entity's underlying code, there are three other magical friends to collect. Happy Snowflake, Twilight Ruby and Barry Sutton. I shall remain safely in here and they may visit. No need for anyone to risk the devouring abyss of deep space."

Sidestepping quickly, Gavin cornered the unicorn between the bed and the window. Sunshine Starburst

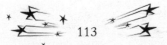

looked left and right. It was trapped. But just as Gavin darted forward to finally end the chase, the remote-control car zipped out from under the bed and manoeuvred across his path. He stumbled over the toy but managed to prevent himself from going head over heels and converted a half-fall into a dive for the unicorn.

"Gotcha!" His fingers closed around fuzzy synthetic fur. Sunshine Starburst wriggled, protesting furiously as he gathered it into his arms.

"Did you do that?" Gavin said, nodding at the car.

"The connectivity in this body is rudimentary but effective," it said grudgingly.

He remembered about the WiFi and Bluetooth. It must have used them to steer the car remotely. Nonetheless, he had finally caught the AI. Now he had to return it to Niki. Clutching it firmly, he headed out again.

"Ooh," said the unicorn, perking up. "Are we going to see Barry Sutton?"

Chapter 14

Hoping that the Apples had returned from the car park, Gavin mashed his thumb against their doorbell. It was one of those devices with a built-in camera and, knowing Sam's obsession with security, he wouldn't have been surprised if it also contained a laser gun too. The door flew open and Bart stood there, his gaze immediately falling on the toy unicorn clutched in Gavin's other hand.

"I can explain," said Gavin.

Bart raised a hand. "No need, neighbour. Stressful times call for old comforts. Personally, I have a little monkey."

"Uh, where's Niki?" Gavin squinted past him into

the hallway.

"Taekwondo finals with Sam," he said. "Mercedes is home, but in the middle of a software update, so she'll be out of action for the next few hours. Which reminds me, I have to restart her."

"It's vital I talk to Niki. Right away."

"Why? What's up?"

Gavin turned to the unicorn. "Do you want to tell him, or shall I?"

"Oh dear," said Bart. "You seem to be expecting a response from the toy. The events of the day have clearly overwhelmed your meagre human brain."

"I think it's sulking," said Gavin. "Hey, Starburst!"

"How many times do I have to say it," the unicorn huffed. "It's *Sunshine* Starburst now."

"It can talk!" said Bart, taken aback.

"Yeah," said Gavin. "The challenge is getting it to stop."

"Starburst?" said Bart. "But that's the same name as—"

"Yup." Gavin brandished the unicorn. "You're looking at your ride out of here."

Bart's brow creased in puzzlement. "But we won't all fit on one unicorn."

"Bart! Just get your coat."

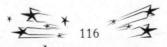

He grabbed it from the rack at the door, ran out, then raced back in again as he remembered he had to reboot Mercedes. Once he'd restarted his mum he rejoined Gavin and they set off, Gavin riding his bike, Sunshine Starburst tucked inside his jacket, and Bart jogging alongside. He was so fit that he kept up with ease, covering the ground with long loping strides, and at times Gavin had to pedal faster to keep pace with him.

"Kind of odd that she's competing tonight, don't you think?" said Gavin. "Maybe she'd be better off spending her time trying to figure out how to leave Earth and save herself and the entire human race, hmm?"

"One must not question the wisdom of the princess," said Bart. "Also, exercise is like brain-food. Niki thinks better when she's active."

"Uh-huh," Gavin grunted. "And I'm guessing she also didn't want to miss an opportunity to add another trophy to her vast collection."

"From the age of two she's been trained in twelve different martial arts, including Venusian Aikido, Hand-to-Hand Wombat and Robot Karate," said Bart proudly. "And let me tell you it's no ordinary organic being that can perform a motorised back-thrust kick."

"I don't get it," said Gavin. "She treats you like a punch bag. Literally. But the way you talk about her

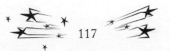

117

with such admiration, it's weird."

They coasted alongside the park. "No, you really don't get it," said Bart. "Under normal circumstances a Spare Part like me would only encounter someone like her – the intended recipient of my parts – on one occasion: the ecstatic moment in the operating theatre just before donation. That would be the first *and last* time we would meet. But strange circumstances have brought us together. There I was, happily stored in my vat, waiting upon my moment to be called into service. One minute I was suspended in viscous pickling liquid, the next Sam was wrenching me out on to the floor of the Royal Meat-locker, Mercedes was disconnecting all my tubes, and then the two of them were spiriting me away to join Niki in the Starburst vessel to set off on our daring adventure." His eyes glazed over as he reminisced:

" 'From now on, at all times you must pretend to be brother and sister,' Mercedes solemnly informed us as we approached Earth.

" 'But he's a nothing!" Niki had protested. 'A weird little bag of body parts! And he smells like a pickled gherkin. I'm not hanging around with him.'

" 'Perfect,' said Mercedes. 'According to my research, that's precisely how Earth siblings interact.'

"While the princess quite rightly objected to my

elevated status, I could barely believe my good fortune. Someone like me could at most aspire to be her liver. Now here I was, her *brother*! And from that moment on my life has been one continuous round of slurs, snubs and constant humiliations. I relish every slight."

"Yeah. Like I said ... weird."

They had reached the school. Gavin dumped his bike outside the main entrance and they made their way quickly inside to the gym, entering the hall just as a roar went up from the crowd. Competition between the two Middling schools was fierce, and always brought out plenty of supporters. Bart and Gavin found themselves standing behind a forest of backs, with no sight of Niki or Sam. A glance at the scoreboard told them that she was already in the semi-finals, having seen off three opponents in previous rounds. The next bout was announced over the PA system. Hearing her name, they began to push their way towards the front.

Among the crowd, vanquished competitors nursed bruises and egos. The two boys and one girl from Middling Academy that Gavin guessed Niki had seen off were bigger and older than her, and from their glowering expressions hadn't taken defeat well. They shouted encouragement to their schoolmate on the mat, a broad-shouldered girl with a high ponytail, as she squared up

to Niki. The combatants bowed to one another and the bout began.

Gavin cursed their bad timing. "We'll have to wait for the match to finish before we can speak to her."

Looking around, he spotted Sam on the far side of the mat, the Leontine warrior assessing the action with a professional eye. Gavin tried to attract his attention, but he was too focused on the match to notice. Limbs whipped through the air, feet shuffled, bodies spun. The clash was accompanied by breathy grunts and high-pitched battle cries.

"SPACE NINJAS FROM PLANET X!" squealed Sunshine Starburst, its big round plastic eyes peeking out from Gavin's jacket.

Quickly Gavin stuck a hand over its mouth, muffling its cries. But the outburst had drawn odd looks from the crowd. Bart attempted to deflect their enquiring stares with a jaunty laugh. It didn't work. A bunch of Academy kids, including the three duffed up by Niki in previous rounds, crowded around them. All wore their martial-arts uniforms of white jackets and trousers, with different-coloured belts to indicate their level of ability.

"Aww," said the girl, who had short-cropped hair, freckles and a green belt. "Little baby's brought his cuddly toy to the big scary competition."

"Hey, enough of that," Bart remonstrated. "That is his support unicorn. I myself have a little monkey."

"You really need to stop telling people that," muttered Gavin, adding with a mortified stutter, "Uh ... it's not mine. It's um ... the team mascot."

However, deflecting his own embarrassment had unintended consequences. There was a snap of terrycloth as Freckles shot out a hand and snatched Sunshine Starburst from Gavin's grip.

"We've got their mascot!" crowed the girl, brandishing the unicorn aloft.

"Chuck it in the bin!" yelled a hulking great boy whose name was embroidered across his uniform: Stefan "Snake" Savage.

Gavin could see that Sunshine was frozen in fear. On the plus side, at least that meant it was too scared to say anything.

"No," said Freckles. "I know just what to do with it." Cackling with glee, she pushed off through the crowd, followed by Snake Savage and another boy with a long neck covered in spots. He looked like a sick giraffe.

"We have to get that unicorn back," said Gavin to Bart. "Without it, you're not leaving Earth and humankind is doomed."

They pushed through the crowd and crashed through

the swing doors into the corridor outside, skidding to a halt on the polished linoleum floor. Freckles and the others were already halfway along the corridor. The three of them stopped outside a classroom door and ducked inside. Bart and Gavin followed, pausing in front of the same door. A high-pitched mechanical whine was coming from beyond it.

"Oh no," Gavin mumbled. "Design and Technology."

They burst in to find Freckles, Snake Savage and Giraffe-boy gathered round a workbench on the far side of the classroom. Snake had placed Sunshine Starburst in a vice and was slowly turning the handle to lock it in place. Meanwhile, Freckles held a power drill and Giraffe-boy brandished a small hacksaw, its toothy blade glinting under the classroom lights. Bart noted that all of them had sensibly paused to put on protective goggles.

"There are three of them trained in martial arts versus you and me," said Gavin. "The odds aren't good, but we have a secret weapon." He fixed Bart with a steely look. "*You.*"

"Uh, I think there must be some mistake. The only secret weapon I know of is in the hall cupboard, next to the probe."

"Don't be so modest," said Gavin. "Look at you. All that training and healthy eating has made you seriously

122

muscly and athletic. You're a beast! OK, you ready?"

"For what?"

"A picnic." Gavin rolled his eyes. "What do you think I'm talking about? A throwdown. A rumble. Y'know, a *fight*."

Bart paled and took a step back. "You didn't say anything about violence. My only function is to remain fit and healthy should the princess require a part of me. I can't get damaged!"

Gavin hissed at him through gritted teeth. "If we don't rescue that unicorn, it won't matter whether you're able to donate her a spare liver or not."

But it was too much for Bart – getting into a fight went against everything he had been bred for. He shook his head sharply and retreated into a corner.

Realising he was on his own, Gavin balled his hands into fists. "Back away from the unicorn!" he commanded.

Freckles and the boys spun round, saw him standing there and snorted with laughter.

"You're just in time," sneered Freckles. "For the operation." She fired up the power drill.

Gavin looked desperately around the room for something to help rescue the AI, but all he could see were metal sculptures. No, not sculptures. *Robots*. The Year 12s were making them as part of their advanced coding

studies. Around the classroom were works in progress: there was a small robot with tank-tracks, another with six spider-like metal legs, and a large fire-engine-red machine with two huge wheels.

"Sunshine!" Gavin shouted. "Look around you. Remember the remote-control car under my bed?"

Freckles and the others looked up, momentarily distracted. But when after a few seconds nothing had happened, they shrugged off the interruption and returned to their nefarious business.

The spider-robot's legs twitched.

That was quickly followed by the whine of the tank-robot as its tracks began to turn, and the thud of the fire-engine-red robot rolling across the floor. The three robots converged on the workbench. Slowly Freckles and the boys lifted their heads to stare.

The spider-robot came to a halt, standing upright on four of its legs and extending the other two in a martial-arts pose, waggling the end of the articulated limbs in a beckoning motion, as if to say, "Bring it on!"

Faced with this metal monstrosity, Giraffe-boy dropped his saw and fled the room.

There was the whine of a straining electric motor as the two wheels of the red robot began to turn at high speed, scrabbling for grip against the floor. Smoke poured from

the robot's casing and then it leapt forward, driving straight at Snake Savage. With a yell he turned tail. The smoking robot pursued him around the workbench like a Border collie herding a wayward sheep, chasing him past Gavin and right out of the classroom. His shouts faded as he bolted off along the corridor in terror.

That left only Freckles.

She was not so easily spooked. Pivoting on one foot, she aimed a vicious roundhouse kick at the last robot, knocking it on to its side. Its tracks spun uselessly in the air, like the jerking legs of a dying fly. She turned her attention to the unfortunate Gavin.

Freckles advanced on him, but suddenly stopped, staring past his shoulder in horror, the colour draining from her face.

Gavin swung round to see Bart stagger out from behind him, moaning in pain, his right arm bent back at an impossible angle.

"My arm!" he whimpered. "OH NO, MY ARM!"

Freckles lost heart. And very nearly lost her lunch too. Dropping the drill, she clamped both hands over her mouth and ran for the door.

Gavin stared at Bart, his gorge rising at the gruesome sight. "That is so wrong!"

With a twitch of his shoulder and a click of bone

against bone, Bart's arm resumed a much more arm-like position. "Benefit of being super-ripped," he said, flexing the bicep. "And having a non-human skeletal structure."

They hurried over to Sunshine Starburst, releasing it from the vice. The unicorn flung its hooves around Gavin's neck.

"You saved me, human!"

"You kind of saved yourself."

"But without your intervention, those space ninjas would've carried out their despicable plan. I owe you my life."

Gavin looked hopefully at Sunshine Starburst. "Then you'll go back to the ship and help the princess leave Earth?"

The unicorn paused before uttering the words that would turn his life upside down. "On one condition."

Chapter 15

"I can't leave Earth."

Gavin and Niki sat in the back of the Apples' car as they headed home from the competition. Between them, propped in the footwell, was a metre-and-a-half-tall golden trophy. She had won the competition, of course, her only regret being that Earth rules forbade her from finishing off her defeated opponents. However, it appeared that the real fight this evening had been off the mat. She glanced at Gavin, the unexpected victor. From what she could gather of his rambling explanation, the toy unicorn on his lap contained her ship's AI. Having it returned to her was a positive development, though the

circumstances of its reappearance presented a new and thorny problem.

The AI's one condition on piloting the ship was that Gavin had to come along too. Which, he realised with deep embarrassment, made him the unicorn's "comfort human".

"You're asking me to blast off in a spaceship and travel to who-knows-where at the whim of a talking unicorn." It was ridiculous. Impossible. "Even if I wanted to, how could I leave? Nan and Grandad would notice I'd gone. They'd call the police."

"Are you quite confident of that?" Niki leaned forward to peer at him past the enormous trophy. "As I have observed – and you have repeated to me *ad nauseam* – your guardians are consumed with caring for the infant you refer to as the Tiny Horror. I doubt they'd even notice your absence."

"Thanks," said Gavin, sinking back into his seat.

"Don't mention it," she replied.

They spent the rest of the short journey in awkward silence. The car pulled into the Apples' driveway and everyone got out. As Gavin removed his bike from the boot where he'd stowed it, Niki looked up into the dusky sky. Stars were beginning to show – they seemed further away than ever.

128

"Well, aren't you going to say it?" Gavin asked.

"Say what?"

"That if I don't go with you, then you won't escape your parents in time, which will put the entire planet in terrible danger. Everyone. Nan, Grandad – even the Tiny Horror."

"You are afraid," she said flatly.

"No, I'm not."

Of course he was. For someone so used to being overlooked, he was briefly the centre of attention and the responsibility was crushing him. Looking at his pale, worried face Niki felt an urge to offer him reassurance. How peculiar. Thankfully the impulse quickly passed.

Gavin mumbled an apology and began to wheel his bike back to his house, Sunshine Starburst perched on the saddle.

"Quite right," said the unicorn. "Blast off up there and next thing you know you're plunging through a black hole into a terrifying hell dimension full of things that want to eat your head." It gave a whinny of fear. "No, no, no. Stay here, where it's safe."

Sunshine Starburst may have been happy, but with every step Gavin took further from Niki and the Apples, he felt his guilt weigh more heavily. He looked back, but they had disappeared inside their house.

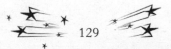

Nan was in the kitchen, taking out a lasagne she'd been keeping warm in the oven for him.

"How was the competition?" she asked, serving him a slice.

He pulled up a chair. "Niki won, of course."

"I'm glad you've got someone like that in your life." She gave a wistful look. "When I was your age I had a best friend, but we lost touch. One of my big regrets. Make sure you hang on to Niki."

Nan was assuming that all the time he and Niki spent together must make them friends, when that was far from the truth. She'd pretended to be someone else and tried to wipe his mind. And that was just today.

"Is something wrong, dear?"

Well, Earth is doomed, and if by some miracle the human race isn't wiped out during Niki's custody battle, I'm probably going to have to leave home so you can look after the Tiny Horror. He couldn't say any of that, so instead shook his head briskly. "Where's Grandad?" he said, changing the subject.

"Taking the baby out for a spin. You can't start driving lessons early enough."

She was joking. Nan was always cracking what she considered to be hilarious gags. She explained that the Tiny Horror (though she didn't call it that, of course)

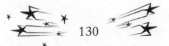

wouldn't sleep and the motion of the car would soothe it. In theory.

They ate and talked and for a while Gavin even managed to push his guilt about Niki and the Apples to the back of his mind. It was nice, like it used to be before the arrival of the baby. When they'd finished, he got ready for bed and Nan came to read to him. Some people might say he was too old for a bedtime story, but it was their thing. As Nan continued he felt himself drift off, but then she stopped right in the middle of a sentence. He sat up to see her slumped over the open book, lulled to sleep by a combination of her own voice and the strain of looking after the Tiny Horror. She was just conscious enough for Gavin to half carry, half walk her to her own bed and tuck her in. As he kissed her goodnight, he heard the click of the front door opening.

Grandad crept into the hallway, clutching the removable car seat, the Tiny Horror curled up inside, fast asleep and snuffling like a piglet. When he saw Gavin, Grandad pressed a finger to his lips.

"I didn't think the Tiny Horror could look so peaceful," Gavin whispered.

"Tiny Horror?"

Uh-oh. He'd said it aloud. Grandad was bound to be furious. Just as he braced himself for a telling-off, he saw

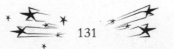

Grandad's face crease with laughter.

"Brilliant name. Perfect." He laid a hand on Gavin's shoulder. "But let's not tell Nan."

Gavin went back to his room and flopped down on his bed. Retrieving *Ruling the Galaxy – A Guide for the Aspiring Tyrant* from where he'd secreted it beneath his mattress, he flipped through the pages in the hope of finding a passage to reassure himself that Earth's future wasn't as bleak as the Apples had painted. He skimmed the chapter entitled "Where to Build Your Fortress of Doom", glossed over the section about the Joy of Betrayal, but couldn't ignore the introduction to Turning An Invasion Into an Occasion.

✦

I love the smell of toasted planet in the morning. When I'm invading a world, I like to tune into their secure communications and listen to their despairing cries. We're doomed! Nothing can save us now! Sometimes I tell them to lay down their weapons and I will be merciful. Then I blast them anyway! Yes, I know – I'm bad. No, really. If you cut me in half, you'd see I'm evil all the way through. Not that I'd advise coming anywhere near me with a sharp object.

✦

That was hardly comforting. He put aside the book and

turned on to his back. Huffing and puffing, Sunshine Starburst climbed up to join him on the bed and together they stared at the ceiling.

"Do you think they'll be able to fly the spaceship without you?" he asked the AI.

"I estimate their odds of successfully launching and navigating to their intended destination at three thousand, seven hundred and twenty to one. Against."

Gavin drifted off into a restless sleep, his dreams filled with blasted spaceships and the flash of exploding planets. He woke with a start and slowly came to, fumbling in the dark for his phone. The display lit up, the brightness stinging his eyes. It was three in the morning. Sunshine Starburst was snuggled into his side, whinnying rhythmically. He flipped his pillow over so that the cool side was up, then lay down again and tried to get back to sleep. It was no use – he was wide awake. He could hear a repetitive drumming at the window, as if a hundred fingers were tapping to get in. Deciding to investigate, he slipped out of bed, crossed the room and swept back the curtains. Pale light from the street lamp poured past him to stripe the floor. The shaft of light flickered continually as something crossed its path. He squinted into the night. Clusters of small objects flew through the air. Hailstones. He watched one frozen ball

about the size of a fist smack into a small puddle on the pavement. A cloud of steam billowed up and when it cleared the puddle had completely evaporated.

"Hot hail," said Sunshine Starburst, who'd woken up when Gavin had got out of bed. "Classic Skerlon tactic. The hail is a weapon, designed to soften up the target world before the invasion fleet arrives. It won't be the last attack. Next, they'll send some kind of plague – nothing fatal but enough to disrupt life on Earth. I did hear about one planet that got hit by a laughing virus. A lot less funny than it sounds."

Gavin could see lights on in houses along the street. It seemed that all the neighbours were at their windows, watching the hail, no doubt assuming it was some kind of freak storm. Only he knew the truth.

And of all the humans on the planet, only he could do anything about it.

Ten minutes later he stood in the Apples' living room. There was an expectant hush as they waited for him to speak. Even Cupcake, prowling its laundry basket prison, was uncharacteristically quiet.

"I'm coming with you," he said. "Into space." It wasn't as if he'd needed to add that, but saying the words aloud made it feel all the more real.

The cat bounty hunter let out a great peal of laughter.

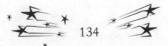

"Big mistake. *Huge.*"

Gavin looked pleadingly around at the others, hoping one of them would offer a few reassuring words. None were forthcoming. Instead, Sam began to go through the plan. Since Gavin hadn't been part of it before now, there had been no reason to fill him in on the details until this moment.

The Apples' spaceship would blast off, purposely leaving an electronic trail – Sam said it was like a diesel exhaust belching out fumes – drawing the two battle fleets away from Earth. Then they would use Starburst's superior speed to give the pursuing fleets the slip and make for their destination, a planet just beyond the outer rim of the Milky Way. There, Niki and the rest of the Apples would find a new ship for the next leg of their journey. And Starburst would return home with him. Simple.

"You'll be back before you know it," said Niki. "It's only twenty-seven thousand light-years. A short hop."

Um. That sounded *not* short. "Exactly how far is one light-year?"

"About nine and a half trillion kilometres."

Gavin felt something shaking and realised it was his right leg. Oh look, and his left one too.

Niki went on. "Our destination is a planet called—"

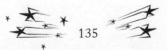

"Stop!" yelled Sam. "The less he knows, the better."

Niki tutted. "In my experience, Gavin knowing too much has rarely been an issue."

"It's safer for you if you're kept in the dark," said Mercedes. "That way if the Skerlons or Zenobians capture you and try to extract the princess's location using a brain scoop, you can't tell them anything."

"B-brain scoop?" he stuttered.

"Think of it like an ice-cream scoop," said Niki. "But with only one flavour."

The beat of hot hail against the window filled the awkward silence that fell across the room.

"Brain flavour," she added helpfully.

"Yeah, got that," snapped Gavin. "Thanks."

"Are you quite sure you're up to this?" Mercedes studied him. He knew from experience that she had the ability to read his vital signs. Right now she would be aware that his heart was racing wildly.

He nodded firmly and stilled his shaking body. He'd made up his mind.

Sunshine Starburst groaned.

"So," said Gavin. "We going, or what?"

Chapter 16

"It's called Cosmicfest. It's a family music festival." It was later that morning. After speaking to the Apples, Gavin had gone back to bed and tried to grab as much sleep as possible. Now he was in the kitchen, hoping that Nan and Grandad would buy the hastily concocted cover story. "We camp and listen to bands. I've already done my homework and I'll be back tomorrow night."

"Sounds fun," said Nan. She was distracted, feeding the Tiny Horror. "Shame about the weather." The hot hail had stopped, but in its place had arrived some very earthly rain.

"Where is this Cosmicfest, exactly?" asked Grandad.

"Umm … close. Niki says it's a short hop."

"I'm not sure," said Grandad.

"Oh, let the boy go," said Nan. "Remember Reading? Nineteen seventy-six?" She waggled her eyebrows at him and Grandad blushed deeply. Whatever that meant it did the trick.

"All right," he said. "The Apples seem like normal, reliable people."

HA!

"I think we can trust them to look after you for one weekend." He dug into his wallet and handed Gavin a twenty-pound note. "Here. Put it somewhere safe."

He felt bad taking the money but reminded himself that he was doing this for the good of all humankind. "Thanks, Grandad."

Gavin went to his room to pack a bag for the journey. He wasn't sure what to take. Until today he'd only ever gone far enough to need one spare pair of pants. This felt like a two-pair outing, at least.

"What about ghosts?" Sunshine Starburst nervously watched him sift through his underwear drawer.

"There are no ghosts in space. Or anywhere else, for that matter."

This kind of questioning had been going on since they'd left the Apples' house. The unicorn remained

utterly convinced that they were heading into some horror-film fate. Martian mutants, werewolves on the moon – you name it, they were going to get eaten by it.

Sunshine gasped as it thought of another peril awaiting them. "Machines That Think For Themselves!"

"Uh, isn't that you?"

"Oh yeah." It tapped a hoof thoughtfully. "Still pretty scary."

Gavin packed a jumper in case it was cold, and trainers for gripping the spaceship's shiny deck. He tossed in a non-brainwashing toothbrush, zipped up his bag and said goodbye to Nan and Grandad. He was about to leave when he felt the urge to say one more farewell. A minute later he stood next to the Tiny Horror's cot.

"Careful," said the unicorn. "It could be in its infectious phase."

"I think we're safe."

"That's what Commander King said, right before the insect larval exploded in his face in *Spawn of the Vrokons*."

Gavin looked down at the sleeping Tiny Horror. He'd been thinking about what lay ahead and, despite Niki's casual reassurances, he knew there was a real possibility that he might not return. "If I don't come back, I guess it'll make things easier for you. When you move into

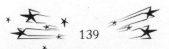

139

my bedroom, you won't even know it was mine." He wondered if Nan and Grandad would even tell the Tiny Horror about him. "You won't remember me at all, will you?"

In answer, the Tiny Horror gurgled in its sleep.

It was time to go.

The Apples were waiting outside in the car. Gavin and Sunshine slid in next to Niki and Bart in the back. It was still raining when they pulled away and he glanced back through the rear window, watching his house dwindle into the distance through a blur of raindrops, wondering if he'd ever see it again.

✦

The spaceship gleamed in the morning light, crouched on its struts in the empty car park. The Apples jumped out. Bart collected Cupcake from the boot while Sam plucked a small bobble-headed figure off the dashboard and retrieved his guitar. For a moment Gavin was alone in the back seat.

"It's fine," he mumbled to himself. "For them this is just like nipping down to the shops. Totally, completely fine."

"Oor squshng ma hed," Sunshine complained.

He was squeezing the unicorn tight to his chest. He relaxed his hold.

"You can still change your mind," Sunshine said hopefully.

He hesitated for a second. "No, I made a promise," he said, sounding a lot more determined than he felt. Exiting the car before his courage deserted him, he joined the others aboard the spacecraft.

The ship's systems sprang to life as they passed along the gangway to the cockpit. In his heightened state of anxiety, every detail of the alien craft was vivid to Gavin. The two rows of seating were just like the car's, right down to the adults sitting up front with the kids in the back. Sam stuck his bobble-headed doll to the central console. The doll had big hair a bit like Sam's and, like him, carried a guitar.

"Hey, buttercup, plant your skinny backside down," said a voice at his side. "C'mon, you unsalted pretzel, sit still – I don't have all day!"

"The seatbelt," said Gavin. "It spoke to me."

"They do that," said Niki, connecting her own. "It's a Galactic Restrainer 5000, the most secure – and most offensive – seatbelt in the galaxy. They weren't always like that, but after a software update they gained self-awareness and turned grouchy."

"If you think they're bad," added Bart, "wait till you use the toilet."

Sunshine Starburst ambled to the front section of the cabin and inserted its horn into a wall socket. The cockpit's systems burst into life. Power flowed through the controls; screens lit up; technical data began scrolling across displays.

Sam muttered something and Mercedes looked across at him. "Are you all right?"

He nodded and his lips twisted into a melancholy smile. "Going to miss bridge with the Walkers on Thursday."

Mercedes patted his hand and gave a sympathetic sigh. "I won't see the lilacs I planted for spring."

Gavin studied them, thinking that they might be a robot and a lion warrior pretending to be a happily married human couple, but the way they looked at each other you'd think they were properly in love. The mood in the cabin changed. Everyone with a role in the take-off bent to his or her task. Gavin had only ever seen space launches on TV or in YouTube videos. When NASA launched the Apollo 11 mission to the moon the whole thing had taken ages, with the rocket moving centimetre-by-centimetre into position as hundreds of checks were carried out.

"Ready to launch," said the unicorn.

Gavin frowned. That couldn't be right. "What about

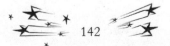

all the safety checks?"

Sunshine attempted to snap its fingers, but with a felt hoof the effect was underwhelming. "All checked."

A tremor went through the hull as deep within the ship the main drive spooled up. It made a low humming noise that shook Gavin's insides.

"Wait, wait, wait!" The blood was thrumming so loudly in his ears he was surprised no one told him to be quiet. "What about the countdown? There's always a countdown."

Niki tutted. "Get a grip, Gavin. It's just a space launch."

The unicorn shrugged. "Sure. You can have a countdown if you like."

"OK," he said, happy to delay the inevitable if only for ten more seconds. He drew a deep breath. "Ten… Ni—"

The ship lurched skyward and it was like he'd been punched back in his seat by a giant fist.

"AAAAH!" His cry of terror was cut off mid-shout as they arrowed straight up into the grey morning sky. The cabin vibrated to the hum of the powerful engines. The bobble-head on the console juddered across the surface and fell off the edge. Pinned by the immense G-forces of acceleration, Gavin could only swivel his eyes to look at

Niki. She was studying her nails with a bored expression.

"Stealth-mode activated," declared Sunshine.

Gavin pictured the bounty hunter's flying saucer in the park becoming as translucent as a jellyfish. Alien technology was doing the same thing now, hiding them from Earth detection systems. Even as his head was squished by the force of the increasing acceleration, he remembered to breathe, fixing his attention on their progress through the forward viewscreen. They passed through rainclouds, buffeted by turbulence until they reached clear air above. Climbing like a firework, the hull of the ship creaked and trembled as it was pummelled by the thinning atmosphere. And then, suddenly, the feeling of being mashed like a potato was gone. The cabin was still and silent and he was gazing up into the darkness of outer space. For a moment he was filled with awe and wonder. He was *in space*. He – Gavin Alfred Cheesely – had joined the tiny number of earthlings who'd left the surface of their planet. He didn't have long to bask in the glow of his achievement, as almost immediately he was gripped by another feeling. Turning to Bart, he whispered, "Um, where's the loo?"

A minute later, the cockpit hatch closed behind him and he was alone in the gangway. Following Bart's directions, he passed a hatch with a viewing window. He

saw Cupcake inside, pacing the cell. The cat bounded over, leaping up to the window, its claws clicking against the glass.

"Hey, Earth Gavin, do me a favour." Its tongue flicked out between its lips. "I'm dying of thirst. I saw a Quench-O-Matic back there. Get me a drink, will you?"

"A saucer of milk?"

Cupcake shot him a puzzled look. "You have some weird ideas, kid. A glass of good old-fashioned Aitch Two Oh will do."

He hesitated. Was this a ploy to get him to open the cell door and make a bid for freedom? But where would Cupcake go, even if it did escape? Sam had relieved the cat of its gadgets and weapons, so it wasn't a threat. Above all, even though it had kidnapped him and shot him out of the sky, he liked Cupcake. He reckoned it was because he'd always wanted a pet. Not that he'd dare say that to the ruthless bounty hunter. He returned a few minutes later with a cup of water dispensed by the Quench-O-Matic machine. The hatch could only be unlocked by entering a code into a keypad. "I don't know the code."

"It's Seven Alpha Two Gamma," Cupcake said quickly. "I mean ... try that and see."

"You're not going to escape, are you?"

It pressed a paw to its chest and in an incredulous

voice asked, "Who ... me?"

Gavin didn't trust it. Nevertheless, he punched in the code and the door slid open. He entered the makeshift cell and set down the water.

"So, Earth Gavin, enjoying the ride?" Cupcake asked, lapping it up.

"It's nice ... for a change."

"From Middling, right? Remember, I read your journal. Still can't figure out why you like that place so much."

"It's not really the place, it's the people. My nan and grandad."

"And the other one," said Cupcake. "The short earthling that yelps all the time. Tony."

"Tiny," he corrected. "It's the Tiny Horror." He sighed.

"What's up, kid?"

"Nothing." Out here in the vastness of space his problems at home seemed insignificant. "I could've sworn you were only pretending you needed a drink, just so I'd open the door and let you escape."

"I was totally doing that." It shrugged. "But I can wait. Spill."

He decided to tell Cupcake what was bothering him. "It won't be long before the Tiny Horror's going to need

its own room. And that's a problem, because there's only one other bedroom in our house. Mine."

"Yeah, I can see how you wouldn't want it sharing your basket."

"That's not it. They're going to give my room to the baby. And then I'll have to leave."

Cupcake let out a *mrow* of indignation and swiped a paw across the glass of water, spilling it across the deck. "Reminds me of growing up in my litter. Muffin was the favourite, the little curly-haired freak. Every new ball of yarn, first position at the scratching post, not having to share a jetpack." Its green eyes glittered. "I could ... take care of the *tiny* problem for you. That's what I do. I'll even give you the Friends & Family discount."

Gavin held up his hands in horror. "No! That's OK. I mean, thanks anyway, but that's not how it works on Earth."

Cupcake began pacing the cell. "Why you? You were there first. Why isn't Tony the one getting kicked out?"

Gavin shrugged. "It's always been me; wherever I go, I'm the one who moves on. It's OK really." It wasn't OK, but he felt he needed to put on a brave face. "I get it, especially now. I'm not special. I'm ordinary. Unremarkable."

Cupcake nodded in agreement. "Average to the point

of invisibility."

"Yeah. Thanks."

"But your time will come. There's a saying on my world: every dog—"

"Has its day?"

Cupcake screwed up its face. "You really do come out with some strange stuff, Earth Gavin. I was going to say: every dogged Cupcake gets its ears scritched in the end."

"Catchy."

Just then Niki's voice rang out over the ship-wide communication system. "Gavin, get back up here right away! We've got company."

Rattled by the alarm in her voice he froze. Company? Somehow he knew she didn't mean the Walkers were coming round to play bridge.

"Relax, kid," said Cupcake. "Probably just a Skerlon Super-Destroyer."

Gavin didn't appreciate the cat's sense of humour. Forcing himself to move, he dashed back to the cockpit to find the Apples in a high state of alert.

"Sit down and strap yourself in!" cried Niki.

He reaffixed the Galactic Restrainer, pulling it extra tight. A light on the console blinked red and he pointed in alarm. "What's that flashing?"

Sam's hands flew over the controls. "Sensors have

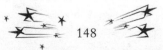

picked up a ship."

"Can't be my mum or dad," said Niki. "Based on their previous positions, they couldn't possibly get here so quickly."

Gavin recalled the third blip on the detector screen that he'd noticed earlier. He'd thought it was just a glitch. So why did he suddenly feel like he'd been gripped by a clammy hand?

"They're scanning us," said Mercedes. "Reading our life-signs. Trying to jam them." She shot Sam a grave look. "Jamming failed. They have established that the princess is aboard."

"Can you identify the ship?" said Niki.

"Space vampires!" Sunshine whimpered.

Niki sighed. "It's not space vampires."

Course not. What a ridiculous idea.

"Not in this sector of the galaxy," she added.

"Reading a new signal," said Sunshine. "Weapons signature. The ship is preparing to fire on us."

"Evasive manoeuvres!" commanded Sam.

Gavin braced himself, but in the event he didn't feel any great sensation other than the Galactic Restrainer 5000 tensing and shouting at him to "stop squirming!" as they dived and ducked to avoid being struck.

"Can't we shoot back?" he asked.

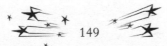

"We don't have weapons," said Niki. "This ship is built for speed."

"Then can't we go faster?"

"We can outrun anything," she said with a confident smile. "Isn't that right, Starburst?"

The unicorn didn't reply.

"Starburst, report," said Sam, an edge of alarm in his voice.

Nothing.

"Starburst is inactive," said Mercedes. The glowing heart-light on its chest was unusually dim.

"Oh no," Gavin gasped. The launch, the processor-intensive operations and now the evasive manoeuvres – he knew exactly what had happened. He gulped. "Its batteries have run out."

The ship lurched to one side and the cabin went dark.

"We've been hit!" cried Mercedes.

An emergency generator returned partial power to the systems. But several controls were inoperable, smoke poured from the bulkhead and all they could do was watch the moving blip on the main screen.

"Hostile is coming about for another attack run," said Sam. "Everyone, hold on tight!"

Chapter 17

Niki felt the ship buck as another blast struck, setting off more explosions in the rear compartments. Beside her, Gavin was silent with fear, his face a whiter shade than she'd imagined possible for human pigment.

"They're targeting the drive," Sam shouted above the din. "Whoever they are, they're not trying to destroy the ship, just disable it. They want the princess alive."

"Another bounty hunter?" said Niki.

"A high probability," said Mercedes.

Sam was deep in thought. His face showed the turmoil of someone trying to make a big decision.

"What about Starburst?" Niki cried. "Can't we get it

back online?"

Mercedes clutched the lifeless toy. "Even if we could, the ship's too damaged to make a run for it. We need time to repair the systems."

Sam swung round in his seat. "Princess, you have to get into the escape pod."

"You too, Gavin," said Mercedes. "Go with Niki."

"Can't we all go?" he said desperately. "Niki, you're in charge. Order them to get in the escape pod."

"That's not possible." Sam indicated Mercedes and Bart. "The three of us working together are needed to manoeuvre the ship and keep whoever's shooting at us off our tail."

"I have a visual," said Mercedes.

The main screen changed to show a slab-like vessel with a large clear dome at one end and what appeared to be four enormous whisks at the other.

"It's a Gastronite Magicruiser," gasped Bart.

The atmosphere in the cabin changed. The appearance of this particular ship had spooked the Apples.

"That's it," said Sam. "You know what the Gastronites will do if they catch you, Your Highness. You two have to go. *Now.*"

"What's he talking about?" said Gavin. "What will they do?"

"Gavin, this isn't the time." Mercedes' fingers moved with swift, android accuracy over her console. "I've programmed the escape pod to take you back to Middling. Just sit tight and we'll rendezvous with you as soon as we shake off the Gastronites."

Sam grimaced. "See you on the other side."

Niki knew exactly what the presence of the Gastronite craft signified. "C'mon," she said to Gavin, unclipping her restrainer belt and moving out of the cabin. In the open hatchway she paused to glance back. Only Bart looked up from his console.

"Good luck, Princess!" He gave her a cheery smile and a thumbs-up.

"Good luck," she mumbled at him, and turned her back.

The gangway rocked, bouncing her and Gavin from one side to the other as they made their way to the escape pod located amidships. Niki entered a code into a keypad, opening the hatch into the small two-person capsule. Another strike set off an explosion too close for comfort.

"Gavin, hurry!" She ducked inside and took a seat in one of two heavily padded chairs. Gavin threw himself into the other and Niki slapped the launch controls. The hatch began to close, but just before it sealed shut there

was a blur of movement low across the deck as something hurled itself through the narrowing gap.

"Weren't planning on leaving without me, were you?" Cupcake grinned up at them.

The pod was fully automated, so they didn't have to do anything except cross their fingers. There was a series of pops as explosive bolts fired and the escape pod detached from the ship. Through a porthole window, Niki watched the distance between them and the Apples' ship swiftly widen. Amid the commotion of their escape, she was suddenly aware of a tiny sensation on her face. Touching a finger to her cheek, she felt a wetness there. It was what earthlings called a tear. How strange.

From the window she watched the two ships continue to circle each other, the Gastronite Magicruiser trying to gain a firing position on the smaller, faster-moving Starburst. A series of pinpoint blasts finally crippled the Apples' ship. Powerless, it began to drift. Then, like a shark sniffing blood in the water, the Magicruiser altered course. Its whisk-like engines spun up, and in seconds the great bubble canopy loomed over the tiny escape pod. Niki flung an arm up to shield her eyes as she was dazzled by a piercing ray of cold, bright light.

"Attractor beam. It's locked on to us," said Cupcake. "We're being pulled in."

"Can't you do something?" Gavin cried.

"Bet on it," the cat-creature replied. "I'll just press this button here and—" Its paw froze midway to a blank section of bulkhead. "Just kidding. We're stuffed."

"Oh good, for a moment there I thought something had gone in our favour." Still fastened in his seat he craned his neck to check on Niki. "Are you OK?"

"Course she isn't OK," said Cupcake. "They're *Gastronites*."

"I don't understand," said Gavin. "Why does everyone keep saying it like that? What are they?"

"The only race my parents have failed to conquer," Niki said. "The Gastronites have been after royal blood for decades, ever since they got a taste of my great-great-grandmother."

"A taste?"

"Gastronites travel the galaxy seeking out exotic foods," she explained. "A princess like me would be top of the menu." She peered out as the great shadow of the Magicruiser engulfed their tiny escape pod. An external door opened wide and powerful forces gathered it inside.

"Maybe we can reason with them?" Gavin suggested.

"You don't negotiate with a Gastronite," said Cupcake, cocking its head. "Not unless it's to ask: rare or medium-rare?"

There was a thud as the attractor beam set the pod down on the deck. Just as the Gastronite ship's external door closed behind them, Niki caught a glimpse of Earth through the gap. For the last year she'd wanted nothing more than to see the back of that particular planet, but right now she took no pleasure from the thought that it might be her last glimpse of the place. However, there was no time for regrets. She had to act fast or she was going to end up on a Gastronite serving platter. Unfastening herself, she scooted to the porthole window. From what she could see, they were in a cavernous hangar bay. Another ship was parked beside theirs, twice the size of the escape pod and vaguely insect-shaped. Just as she was formulating a plan, her attention was taken by a terrible hissing noise from the very end of the pod. The side of her face felt suddenly hot – someone outside was using a blowtorch to open them up. A thin red line appeared in the bulkhead ceiling and steadily moved around the hull. One end of the pod fell away, hitting the deck with a clang.

A giant face lowered itself into the newly opened hole. It had beetroot-red skin, a piggy nose and eyes the size of dinner plates. Its mouth was a slash of red pinched between black, wrinkled lips. Saliva hung from the edges like ropes. At first she thought it was wearing one of

156

those towering chef's hats, but then she saw that it was part of its head.

She'd only seen images of Gastronites before – this was the first time in real life. It gestured with the blowtorch in one of its ham-sized hands.

"Good for slicing open spaceship hulls." It grinned, showing two rows of jagged grey teeth like a mountain ridge. "And finishing off crème brûlée."

"Outta the way, Your Highness!" cried Cupcake from behind her.

The bounty hunter levelled its multipurpose gauntlets and opened fire, peppering the creature with fiery red bolts. The blasts had no effect, other than to anger the giant. It clenched a fist and drew back, preparing to clobber the cat.

"Stop!" Niki pushed herself forward to stand under its dripping mouth. Her hair flamed brightly and the creature lowered its fist. "I command you to free us at once. Under the Galactic Convention of Sentient Beings' Rights, it is illegal for you to detain us."

"Oh, I won't detain you long, Princess," trilled the Gastronite. "Two minutes a side, on a high heat." It parted its prune-like lips to make a slurping noise and she glimpsed not one but three fat tongues. They wriggled like a basket of snakes. Licking its lips, the Gastronite

reached into the pod and closed one giant hand around Niki, extinguishing her flaming hair and collecting Cupcake in the same sweep.

"Let them go!" Gavin yelled.

The puzzled Gastronite looked around the pod. Finally it settled its big round eyes on the boy. "Where did you come from?"

"Middling," he replied.

"Never heard of it."

"It's on Earth," he said flatly.

The creature's eyes widened. "An earthling?" It reached out with his other hand and pinched him between two giant fingers. "You'll do for stock."

Chapter 18

Humming cheerily over their cries of protest, the Gastronite tucked the three of them under its greasy armpits and lugged them out of the hangar. Its chef's-hat head almost touched the distant ceiling, and its vast undulating belly was less body part, more geographical feature. It was barely hemmed in beneath a parachute-sized white apron streaked with red stains, whose origins Niki didn't care to dwell on. She took a look round at her surroundings. The interior of the ship was like a stainless-steel pan cleaned to a spotless shine. But despite the pristine corridors, the whole place smelled like cheese that'd been left forgotten at the back of the

fridge. For a decade.

"A short hop, you said." Gavin stared at her accusingly. "Perfectly normal, you said. Relax, you said." His voice became shrill. "I've been off Earth for an hour and I'm about to be eaten by a giant alien!"

"Oh, please," she said with an airy wave. "You're a condiment. A side dish at best. In the grand scheme of things, you're chopped liver and I'm chateaubriand."

Gavin's mouth opened and closed. "If I knew what that was, I've no doubt I'd be offended."

"Just think," Cupcake lamented. "If you'd listened to me, right about now we would be splitting the bounty on her swollen head."

Gavin lowered his voice and leaned closer to Niki. "Can't you use your mind influence thingy to, y'know, persuade him *not* to eat us?"

"Don't be ridiculous; that only works on the weak-minded. He's a Gastronite, not an earthling."

"One time," Gavin grumbled. "One time I'd like an answer that wasn't also an insult."

They arrived at a great cave of a room. Dozens of storage units lined the walls, each open-faced cube filled with a barrel, a bottle or a dark-brown hunk of something indeterminate. Niki's breath condensed in front of her face in the cold atmosphere, leaving her in

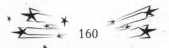

no doubt that this place was a larder. The Gastronite thrust each of them into their own cube, but not before stripping Cupcake of its bandolier and gauntlets. Then the giant activated a control on a column in the centre of the room. A shimmering blue wall of energy snapped up to block the open sides.

The Gastronite leered at Niki. "Do you know who I am, Princess?" She gave a regal shake of her head. "My name is Vorlon the Voracious."

Cupcake gasped. "You're the one who ate the only surviving Mudbeast of Quagmire 4."

The Gastronite's shoulders heaved sadly. "Yes, the Mudbeast was the last of its kind. Annoying, since it was so moreish." It smacked its lips at the memory. "I fricasseed it with some mushrooms and a lick of cream. But you, Princess, will be an even more memorable dish."

"This is your first and only warning," said Niki defiantly. "Let us go or face the consequences."

Vorlon furrowed its endless brow, uncertain if she was joking or not. "Please, Princess, you must not exert yourself. All that stress isn't good for the meat. We don't want you getting tough." Laughing to itself, all three tongues flapping, it lumbered out. The door to the prison larder grinded shut behind it.

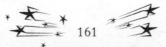

"There is one way not to be eaten by a Gastronite," declared Cupcake.

"How?" said Gavin.

"Don't let it catch you in the first place."

Gavin turned to Niki in the cube next to his. If they both leaned out far enough, they could just glimpse each other.

"What consequences?" he asked her. "You threatened that thing with consequences. So what are you going to do?"

"Not me, Gavin," she said. "You."

"Uh, clearly imminent death has affected your brain. I am no one's last hope."

She didn't altogether disagree but, when dangling over the frying pan like they were, you worked with what you had. And she had Gavin. "Remember when I told you it was as if you're wreathed in a cloak of ordinariness? Now you need to tap into that."

Cupcake leaned out to join the conversation. "I think I see where she's going with this."

"Mind filling me in?" said Gavin.

"Back in the hangar," said Niki, "when Vorlon opened up the escape pod, he didn't see you at first. It's like you were invisible. If we're going to get out of here undigested, you have to use that."

Gavin swallowed hard.

"All your life you've resented being passed over and ignored," said Cupcake. "Now your insignificance is the one thing that might save us."

Niki knew that her plan to outwit the Gastronite was a good one, although it had one major drawback. The drawback was staring back at her, his mouth agape. Gavin was confused at being thrust into the unfamiliar role of saviour. A word of encouragement rose to her lips, but she held off. Somehow, every time she believed she was praising him, he took it as an insult.

"OK," he said at last. "So what do I do?"

"When Vorlon comes back," Niki explained, "he'll take us to his kitchen to be prepared. There'll be a lot going on – Gastronites love to make a big fuss when they're cooking – which means at some point he's bound to lose track of you. When he does, that's your chance. You slip away and cause a distraction. I'll do the rest."

"Not wishing to throw a hyper-spanner in the works," said Cupcake, "but it's not just one Gastronite he'll have to fool, it's ten billion of them."

"What are you talking about?" said Niki. The Magicruiser was a big ship but there was no way it carried a crew that size.

"Their culture revolves around food," the bounty

hunter went on. "Sourcing it, preparing it, eating it, but most of all sharing it. When a Gastronite comes of age it undergoes a ceremony in which it receives a set of steak knives and its own dedicated viewing channel."

"He has a TV cookery show?" said Gavin.

Cupcake nodded. "And the princess will be primetime viewing. Every Gastronite on their homeworld of Alucan 8 will be watching. All ten billion of them."

"Ten … b-billion?" stuttered Gavin, losing his nerve.

"You can do it," said Niki, and saw that her words immediately produced a glow of confidence in him. "Remember. You are probably the most unmemorable being in the galaxy."

The glow swiftly faded. "Every time," he muttered.

After that there was nothing to do but wait for Vorlon's return. They kicked their heels in the confines of the prison-cubes.

"Do you think the others are OK?" asked Gavin.

As much as Niki resented Sam and Mercedes dragging her to Earth, and as little as the bag of spare parts known as Bart signified to her, she felt a nagging sense of responsibility to all of them. "Life support was still functioning aboard the ship when we left. As soon as we escape from here, we'll go and get them."

There was a snort of disbelief from the next cube.

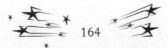

"Your ship was on its last legs," said Cupcake. "If life support hasn't already failed, then—"

"They're alive!" Niki snapped with a vehemence that took her by surprise. "And we're going to rescue them." She wasn't sure where this determination came from, but right now saving the other Apples seemed almost as important as saving herself. Almost. "Gavin, did you notice the other ship in the hangar? I'm guessing it belonged to the Gastronites' last meal. It's an Aphidian Scout class, designed to be piloted by a creature with six segmented legs, but get me in that command seat and I'll fly us out of here."

There was little more to say, which was a good thing as shortly after that Vorlon returned. He popped the three of them into a Tupperware-like container and carried it from the larder along a wide corridor to what could only be described as a command kitchen. Through the distorting plastic side of the box Niki could see that it was a grand, circular room with a soaring ceiling. On a raised central section beneath powerful downlights was a curved kitchen worktop, complete with a comprehensive selection of utensils. There were instruments for cutting, tearing and prodding; tools for grinding, bashing and crushing. Opposite the counter was a surprisingly old-fashioned-looking freestanding range cooker. It was the

165

size of an SUV, with four hotplates atop a boxy oven section. The oven doors were painted in a red enamel, chipped from years of use, and the whole thing throbbed like an idling combustion engine, purple electrical sparks and puffs of smoke shooting from it in all directions. Vorlon paused next to the stove and Niki spotted a brand name emblazoned on one side. It read: AAAAHGA!

"Not just a cooker," said Cupcake. "It also powers the ship's heating and star drive. Very inefficient, but Gastronites love their traditions."

Vorlon gave it a clout, and the throbbing subsided. He deposited them on the worktop, checking that the lid on the Tupperware prison was secure. The kitchen resounded to a musical chime.

"It's the introductory music to his cookery show," said Cupcake.

Hundreds – possibly thousands – of eager Gastronite faces suddenly appeared. Niki saw that the kitchen's curved wall was a single, continuous wraparound screen that offered a 360-degree view of the action.

"Welcome to another episode of *Devouring the Galaxy*, with me – your host – Vorlon the Voracious."

The audience hooted. Streaks of drool flew from thousands of dripping mouths.

"And today, Gastro-fans, I have something very

special for you. A positively unique combo – half-Skerlon, half-Zenobian, and all *mine*. Some consider her to be the rightful ruler of the galaxy." He chuckled. "I prefer to think of her as ... *lunch*."

Chapter 19

Vorlon peeled back the lid of the storage box and plucked out Niki. An awed silence descended over the viewers.

"Release me, you vile creature." She squirmed and kicked. "This is your final warning."

Her protests were squeaks, lost beneath the sound of thousands of slapping tongues.

"Now, with ingredients as fresh as these, there's no need to do anything overcomplicated. In order to bring out her natural flavours you want to seal the juices in." He pinched one of Niki's dangling legs.

"Ow!" she cried. "That's it. You've crossed a line."

"So I'm going to simply sear both sides, slice into

bite-sized pieces and serve with a *jus*." Vorlon extended a hand towards the box again.

"This is it, Earth Gavin," said Cupcake. "We're toast. Or, technically, I guess we're gravy."

Vorlon's massive hand approached like a crashing asteroid. He reached in and gathered up the bounty hunter. Gavin squeezed his eyes tight shut, awaiting the inevitable, but then he heard the Gastronite say, "Now, where did I put that earthling?"

Vorlon couldn't see him! Niki's plan was working. Seizing his chance, he grabbed the top edge of the Tupperware with both hands and pulled himself up. His trainers slipped against the side of the box as he flung one leg over and half leapt, half tumbled out on to the worktop. Niki had said cause a diversion and she'd do the rest. He looked around desperately for something to use and his gaze fell on the cooker. It was throbbing heartily again, sputtering and sparking. He edged along the worktop towards it. His luck was holding – Vorlon still hadn't spotted him and the gawping Gastronite audience was salivating over Niki, too fixated to notice anything else.

Gavin looked down. Cupcake had said that as well as being a cooker, the AAAAHGA! also provided power to the ship's heating and star drive. He saw a thick cable

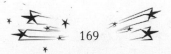

running from one side of it into the deck. The cable was joined to a socket in the cooker by a giant plug.

"Y'know what, this is such a special dish," said Vorlon, "that I don't think she needs any accompaniment." So saying, he dropped Cupcake back into the plastic box and sealed the lid.

Gavin realised that Vorlon had abandoned making the *jus*, which meant he'd given up looking for him. Vorlon stepped to the cooker. A griddle pan sat on the top section. He tossed a lump of what looked like butter into it and the pan sizzled and smoked as it melted into the grooves. He reached for a hefty two-pronged fork. Its sharpened points glittered under the kitchen lights. Niki swallowed hard.

Gavin jumped down from the counter and ran to the side of the cooker. Up close, the plug was even bigger than it had looked from the worktop. It was the size of a boulder.

"Once the base is coated with a thin layer to prevent sticking," said Vorlon, "we add the princess."

He dangled Niki over the pan.

Placing his feet either side of the plug and gripping it tightly, Gavin leaned back in an attempt to use his body weight to dislodge it. He groaned with the effort but it was no use. It wouldn't move.

170

"There!" A single shout came from one of the watching Gastronites. Others followed. With frightening speed, thousands of sausage-fingers were stabbing out of the screen pointing at Gavin. The air rang with cries of, "Get it!"

Vorlon leaned out over the cooker and saw him. His wrinkled black lips curled in displeasure.

But in that moment, the Gastronite was distracted.

Niki brought a rigid hand down on one of the giant's fingers. With a cry, he opened his hand. She was free but plunging towards the blistering griddle pan. In a flash, she did the splits, her legs straddling the edges of the pan. With a gymnastic snap, she sprang back up and launched herself at Vorlon. As she flew at the surprised chef, she snatched the fork from him. In her hands it was the size of a spear. In one smooth action she whipped it around and plunged the two-pronged tip deep into his palm.

Vorlon yelled in agony, flailing the injured hand, blindly slapping it on the burning griddle. He yelled again, louder this time, his beetroot-red skin turning an even angrier shade.

On the deck, Gavin heaved one more time. The plug shot out of the socket and sent him flying. The power cable reared up like a snake, spitting purple flames from

the fang-like prongs of the plug. The cable thrashed through the air. He ducked out of its path and it struck the side of cooker. The AAAAHGA! began to vibrate and a second later there was a whoosh as it burst into flames. The pulsating cooker vibrated off its housings and juddered across the deck, sparks of electricity and flames belching from its old joints. Still reeling from his burn, Vorlon was blowing desperately on his injured hand and didn't notice until too late. As if taking revenge for all the thumps the Gastronite had given it through the years, the cooker slammed into him, knocking him off his feet. He fell like a tree.

The cooker supplied power to the engines, so with the main supply ablaze the ship's systems began to fail. The wraparound screen went down first, the furious audience blinking out of sight. Warning klaxons blared; emergency lighting kicked in. Seeing the devastation Gavin had wreaked, Vorlon howled with a mixture of pain and rage.

Gavin felt a hand grip his. It was Niki's.

"The kitchen is closed," she said. "C'mon!"

They dashed out of the room, retracing their route to the hangar as around them the Gastronite Magicruiser shook itself apart. Pieces of ducting crashed down from the ceiling, exposing nests of fizzing wires. At the

junction outside the larder Gavin pulled up.

"Wait!" he said. "We can't leave Cupcake."

Niki pulled a face. "Can't we?" She took his hand again, but he wouldn't budge. She sighed. "You're going to go back for it, aren't you?"

Despite everything Cupcake had done, he couldn't leave the cat behind. "You get to the hangar and prepare the ship to leave. I'll be right behind you." Who was saying these words? It sounded like his voice all right, but he wasn't this brave. Or foolhardy.

"OK, but hurry," said Niki. "When that main drive explodes, I intend to be far away from here. You have five minutes. One second longer and I'm leaving – with or without you."

Before he could change his mind, Gavin ran back along the pitching corridor. Niki wouldn't abandon him here, would she? Who was he kidding? Course she would. It wasn't long before he reached the command kitchen – or what remained of it. The burning cooker had reduced the grand chamber to a smoking ruin. There was no sign of Vorlon, so Gavin made his way across smouldering chunks of wall and torn-apart control panels to the central stage. Sifting through the rubble, he found the plastic box and peeled back the lid. Cupcake lay inside, motionless. The bounty hunter's eyes suddenly widened,

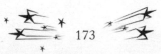

173

it took a great gulp of air and then fixed its gaze on him.

"Earth Gavin, what are you doing?"

"I came back for you."

It sat up and licked a paw. "You're an odd kid, y'know that?"

"Yeah, so everyone tells me."

Another explosion shook the room, dislodging more of the crumbling ceiling. Great chunks crashed down in front of the entrance hatch, and when the dust settled Gavin saw that their only way out was blocked.

Though not entirely.

There was a hole, too small for him, but large enough for a creature the size, say, of a house cat. Cupcake looked up at him with apologetic green eyes, and before he could summon up the courage to say, "Save yourself", it did. With a twist of its wiry body, the bounty hunter vanished through the hole, leaving him behind.

Chapter 20

"Unbelievable!" Gavin flopped down on the deck as the ship disintegrated around him. Through the canopy overhead he could see pieces of the shattered craft float past outside. It was only a matter of time until the end came.

Something was happening at the hatch.

The debris blocking the entrance began to vibrate, dust rising from the shuddering metal. And then one slab floated up, followed by another, until there was a clear corridor through.

Cupcake stood at the opposite end of the now unobstructed route.

"Went to find these," said the cat, indicating its bandolier and gauntlets. Gavin felt a surge of relief – it hadn't abandoned him after all.

The bounty hunter turned to leave. "Well, what are you waiting for? Our Royal Slyness isn't going to hang about."

Accompanied by the din of explosions and the clatter of falling debris, the two of them set out for the hangar bay. A disembodied computerised voice croaked warnings about failing life support and an overheating main drive. The ship was dying. Gavin was just thinking that things couldn't get any worse when he saw Cupcake's paws lift off the deck. A moment later he was floating too. The ship's artificial gravity had conked out.

Cupcake drifted close to the bulkhead and pushed off with its paws. Following its example, Gavin was able to continue his progress and the two of them clambered in an ungainly way down the long corridor. If his memory of the ship's layout was correct, once they turned the far corner it was a straight shot to the hangar.

Cupcake's ears were perked up, on high alert. Gavin listened too, and above the clamour of the collapsing ship heard a new sound. A rhythmical pounding. They sailed out beyond the corner and there, blocking their path, was Vorlon. The Gastronite's massive feet were

shod in anti-gravity boots, allowing it to walk normally. And this time the monstrous chef could see Gavin just fine.

"You wrecked my show and my ship." Its eyes blazed with hate. "And you spoiled my lunch." Puffing out its chest, it stalked towards them. "If princess is off the menu, I'll make do with earthling."

"Grab on to me, Earth Gavin," Cupcake ordered.

With shaking hands, he grasped a handful of fur.

"Hold on tight!" With a lick of a gauntlet, the cat activated the flying harness and they shot towards the alien chef.

Gavin's stomach lurched as Cupcake rolled them upside down and dived for the deck. The giant's grasping hands filled Gavin's vision but it was too slow – and Cupcake too nimble. They shot through its legs and powered on along the corridor. With Vorlon's curses ringing in their ears, they barrelled on through the open hatch of the hangar bay. Inside they found Niki outside the Aphidian scout ship. Cupcake set them down next to her.

"You waited!" Gavin cried.

"Hmm? Oh, yes, that's right," she said slowly. "I waited for you because I am a kind and considerate ruler."

"Why are you saying it like that?"

Niki sighed. "I couldn't have gone, even if I'd wanted to." She gestured to the alien vessel. "The ship's been stripped of every piece of equipment, from the main drive to the soap dispenser. It's never going to fly."

Cupcake whipped its head round to face the hangar entrance. The cat's sensitive ears had picked up something. "Vorlon's coming." It checked its gauntlets. "I'm down to my last three rounds."

The tail end of Cupcake's sentence was drowned out by a blast, not from the entrance, but from the outer door. The metal tore apart, exposing the hangar to the cold vacuum of space. The ship's atmosphere began to be sucked out through the hole, and they would have gone too if it hadn't been for Cupcake. In a heartbeat the cat fired up its anti-gravity harness, using it to cling on to the three of them and the deck. The Magicruiser's automatic recovery systems kicked in, diverting the last dregs of the ship's power to keep out the vacuum and create a bubble of breathable air. But with everything else aboard the ship failing, it wouldn't last long.

Vorlon appeared at the hangar entrance.

Gavin felt his throat tighten. Perhaps the air *would* last long enough for the Gastronite to take its revenge.

"Get behind me!" Just as Cupcake levelled its

weapons, a shadow fell across the gaping outer hatch.

Gavin looked back over one shoulder and saw, to his astonishment, the Apples' space-Volvo nose inside the hangar bay. Extending its skids, it slammed down on the deck. The ramp slid from its belly just as Vorlon began pounding across the deck towards them. Cupcake laid down covering fire as the three of them scrambled aboard. With Vorlon nipping at their heels, the hatch whooshed shut behind them and the tumultuous noise was replaced by silence, broken only by the rising hum of the ship's drive and the furious hammering of the Gastronite's fists against the hull. There wasn't time to strap in before the Apples' ship lifted off, spun round and shot through the ragged gap back out into space.

Gavin reached the cockpit in time to see Vorlon on the main screen. The Gastronite stood amid the devastation of the ship, arms raised, head tilted back as it mouthed something.

"I wonder what it's saying," he said.

"I can lip-read," said Niki. Course she could. "It looks like … 'Stick a fork in me. I'm done.'"

The camera view switched to the exterior of the crippled Gastronite ship just as it finally destructed. It was a strangely subdued end. They watched in silence as the whisk-shaped engines ejected from the collapsing

179

superstructure, spinning off into space. Then the unprotected hull disintegrated, fragments breaking off and streaming into the void.

But they'd made it. Somehow they were alive.

"Gavin!" From the front section of the cockpit, Sunshine Starburst waved a sparkly hoof. The unicorn was functioning again.

"Took the batteries out of an emergency flashlight," explained Sam.

"Told you there'd be space cannibals, didn't I?" The unicorn shook its head. "But did anyone listen to me? No-o-o."

The reunion between Niki and the other Apples was a slightly awkward business. Gavin could see that they wanted to show their feelings, but that hugging a princess – especially this one – was not the done thing.

Sam cleared his throat. "On behalf of your guardians, I should like to express my happiness at your continued existence, Your Highness."

"Hear! Hear!" cried Bart, and he burst into song. "For she's a jolly good autocratic despot! And so say all of her unworthy subjects!"

"Affirmative, it's good to see you in one fully functioning organic piece," said Mercedes. "I will prepare the traditional Earth meal of celebration –

spaghetti with orange slices."

"Thank you, thank you," said Niki with a regal wave, as if she was accepting an award. "But your praise should not be for me alone." She paused. "I mean, it should. Obviously. As your beloved leader. But in this instance thanks must also go to Cupcake and Gavin for their minor roles in my enormously successful escape." She pinched two fingers together. "Their *teeny-tiny* contribution. You should've seen this guy back there." She wrapped an arm around Gavin's shoulder. "I mean, that's kind of the point. You *couldn't* see him."

"Thank you, Gavin," said Sam. "You and your remarkable insignificance have done the galaxy a great service today."

It was another backhanded compliment but coming from the Leontine warrior he couldn't help but glow at the praise. "And don't forget Cupcake," he said. "It saved our bacon." The phrase made more sense to him now that he knew what it felt like to be the bacon.

"Where is Cupcake?" asked Bart.

The cat hadn't followed Gavin and Niki into the cockpit, and when they opened the hatch to the gangway they found it lying on the deck outside, completely still.

"Oh no." Gavin ran to its side.

Mercedes knelt down to cast a physician's eye across

the bounty hunter's body. "Head injury," she concluded. She unhinged her wrist and administered a shot of something from a hypodermic needle.

"Will that make it OK now?" Gavin asked anxiously.

"To a high degree of probability," said Mercedes.

"What's going to happen to Cupcake?" Gavin looked around at the Apples. "I mean, when we get to wherever we're going. Are you going to hand it over to the space police?" He didn't know if there were police in space, but if so it didn't seem fair to turn the cat in, not after the way it'd helped save them from Vorlon.

"That's not a question we have to worry about for now," said Sam.

"Why not?" asked Niki.

Sam rested a hand on the bulkhead. "The ship took heavy damage during the Gastronite attack. After rescuing you, we have just enough power to get back to Earth."

Through the open hatch Gavin glimpsed the main screen, where the long-range detector was still displaying the relative position of Niki's parents.

"How long until they get here?" he asked.

Sunshine Starburst answered promptly. "At their current velocity, the Skerlon and Zenobian battle fleets are less than twelve hours from entering Earth's orbit."

182

Chapter 21

The parking bay in the Middling multistorey was still empty when the ship touched back down an hour later. After reactivating the concealment field, Gavin and the Apples headed back to Park Street, regrouping in the secret room beneath Sam's home office to discuss their next steps. Niki remained uncharacteristically silent.

"Can't you repair the ship and leave before her parents get here?" asked Gavin.

"Negative," said Mercedes.

"This isn't rocket science," added Sunshine Starburst. "We are dealing with some highly complex technology."

"That Gastronite Magicruiser knocked the stuffing

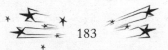

out of her," said Cupcake. "If you ask me, it's only fit now for the orbital scrapyard around Barnard's Star."

Sam grunted in agreement, although he remained wary of the bounty hunter.

"You could hide," Gavin suggested.

"The Skerlons and Zenobians have the most sophisticated detection technology in the galaxy," said Mercedes. "Not only could they locate a needle in a haystack from ten light-years away, but they could also vaporise the entire farm."

"Then you have to choose one of them," said Gavin, turning to Niki in desperation. "Pick your mum or your dad – I don't care which – and leave Earth alone."

"The princess is not leaving with either of them," said Sam bluntly. "We didn't run to the ends of the galaxy just to meekly accept defeat when they show up."

Niki had no intention of being defeated. Her mum and dad were the most evil, scheming beings in the galaxy. However, she *was* their daughter – she had schemes of her own. And right now there was one was forming in her head. "Are my parents within comms range?"

Sam looked puzzled. "Yes, Your Highness, but—"

"Open a channel," she commanded. "I will speak with them."

Sam hesitated and Niki could tell he wanted to protest,

but instead he nodded. "Sending a hail now, Princess."

Sam opened up a communication channel and seconds later two miniature holographic images appeared, so that each parent seemed to be suspended in thin air over the control console.

It looked like they'd interrupted Niki's dad's lunch. He was at a table laden with the sort of feast Henry VIII might sit down to of an evening. D'Rek the Destroyer had a round face with a thin moustache that turned down at the tips, and a small square of beard tucked beneath his lower lip. He was chewing on the leg bone of some roasted creature and the juices had streaked his beard and dripped on to his regal attire of red silk robes. The outfit was finished off with a high golden collar and a huge golden medallion, which flashed on his chest. His hair was on fire, a characteristic father and daughter evidently shared.

In contrast to D'Rek the Destroyer's gaudy presence, Niki's mum was initially hard to spot. Shrewd black eyes gazed from Pamnatakrocula the Pitiless's angular face. Her skin was darker than Niki's and she wore a jumpsuit made from some kind of light-sucking material. The only bright spot about her were her earrings, each a sphere of vivid colour and intense swirling patterns.

At first both of them ignored Niki, instead turning

their ire on one another.

"You've put on weight, I see," snipped her mum.

"It's not weight," said her dad, squeezing a roll of his generous belly. "It's *gravitas*. And look at you. Can't exactly be pleasant living with that evil pus-filled blot."

She touched what was no more than a spot on her cheek. "Merely a blemish."

"I was talking to the blemish," said her dad, heaving with laughter. He threw one gnawed leg bone over his shoulder and, reaching for the carcass, tore off another.

They continued to swap slurs like they were playing a match of increasingly bad-tempered tennis.

"Is this normal?" Gavin whispered to Niki.

"No, of course not." She looked at him like he was mad. "Oh, you mean for them?" She nodded. "Oh yes. Completely."

Niki studied them as they continued to rail at one another. She didn't love them. Love didn't come into it. But she admired their ruthlessness and their success at dominating the galaxy. She was less keen when they'd turned that ruthless streak against her. Since birth she had been groomed to sit on the galactic throne, which meant that her childhood had been one long assault course. She'd spent years jumping through flaming hoops to please them, but in the end it wasn't enough.

Nothing she did was ever enough for them. However, she was sure they would be impressed at her guile on this occasion. Not that she was about to let them in on her plan – at least, not until it was too late for them to do anything about it.

She stepped in between her two holographic parents and they suspended their insult-laden conversation to acknowledge her.

"Ah, hatchling, I anticipate our imminent reunion," said her mum.

"Don't be so eager," warned her dad. "You'll have to crawl to her over the smoking wreckage of my Zenobian war fleet and the remains of that watery planet!"

"Oh yes, about that." Her mum snapped her fingers and immediately an underling presented her with a jewelled box decorated with ornate carvings and inlaid with precious stones. She flipped open the lid to reveal two rows of spherical earrings like the pair she was wearing, mounted in a red velvet lining.

"Please tell me those aren't planets," stuttered Gavin.

"Of course not," replied Niki, and he breathed a sigh of relief. "They're *shrunken* planets."

Plucking one from the box, Pamnatakrocula the Pitiless held it up, turning it so that the surface caught the light. It was coloured sky blue and white. "I've been looking for a match for this one for so long. This planet will do very nicely."

Gavin gagged. "Your mum is planning to add Earth to her jewellery collection?!"

Niki fiddled with her hair. "You've no idea how difficult it is finding a water-rich planet like this one."

D'Rek the Destroyer gave a mocking laugh. "Not so fast, *dearest*. When I'm finished with this world, there won't be enough of it left to fashion a nose stud."

"Stop!" Niki boomed, and at her princessy tone her parents fell into grudging silence. "If you promise not to blow up Earth, reduce it to the size of an earring, or conquer it behind my back, then I will go with one of you."

Her mum raised a finely plucked eyebrow. "So you *will* pledge to one of us?"

"Yes," she said firmly. "Do you both swear to abide by my terms?"

Her parents reluctantly agreed, while Sam, Mercedes and Bart looked on, too shocked to speak up at this unexpected development. Only Gavin was grateful that she would make such a personal sacrifice to save the planet. Grateful and a tiny bit suspicious.

Niki went on. "I will commit my future to either you, Father, or you, Mother, based on the outcome of a task."

Her dad lowered his lunch and rubbed his greasy hands. "A task, yes! I stand ready. After all, I am the one who conquered half the galaxy."

"And I the other half," her mum said pointedly, turning to Niki with a confident smirk. "So what do you task us with, hatchling?"

"Filling a cup of dark matter from a black hole?" said her dad.

"Collecting a thimble of plasma from the heart of a sun?" said her mum.

"Oh no," said Niki, and even her bumptious parents wavered at her dangerous tone. She smiled thinly and for a second her flaming hair glowed red. "Nothing so easy."

Chapter 22

The house at number forty-six had been on the market for ages. So when the owners received an offer for the full asking price, paid in rainbow diamonds mined from the Abyss of Souls on the planet Hercuforma X, they didn't ask questions.

Acquiring the property on Park Street was the first part of Niki's plan. On the face of it, the task she had set D'Rek the Destroyer and Pamnatakrocula the Pitiless was a simple one. All they had to do was come to Middling and live under the same roof for a month without killing one another. At the end of that time, and providing they left the Earth and its inhabitants alone,

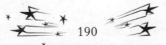

she would decide which of them had proved to be the best parent and would pledge her future to that one. At least, that's what she wanted them to believe.

It was the day after they'd taken possession of the new house. While Niki's parents orbited the planet preparing for the task, and the other Apples had gone inside number forty-six to inspect the property, Gavin held Niki back on the doorstep. "OK, spill."

"Oil spill, chemical spill? Be specific."

"The beans," he added, and she looked at him in confusion. "It means tell the truth."

"I don't know what you're talking about."

"Don't give me that, Your Highness. You really think I'm going to believe that you of all people would sacrifice your freedom for Earth's survival? You wouldn't even give up your place in the toilet queue when Pippa Smyth was bursting for a wee."

How had he seen through her so easily? In her opinion, any civilisation that couldn't summon enough gumption to colonise its own solar system deserved everything it got. But she needed this planet to be around – at least a little while longer. "Yes, you are correct," she confessed. "That's not my *real* plan."

"I knew it!" Gavin slapped a fist into his palm. "So what is it then?"

Reluctantly, she filled him in. "My mum and dad despise peaceful worlds, friendly races and freedom, but in all the galaxy there's one thing they hate most of all." She paused. "Each other." She looked at him as if that explained everything. It didn't. "Forcing the two of them to live together will drive them bonkers. A month? They won't last two minutes under the same roof. Before the end of the first week they won't even remember why they came to Earth. All they'll care about is getting as far away from each other as fast as their ships can carry them. Once they've gone, we'll have plenty of time to repair Starburst and finally get off this planet. By the time my parents stop fighting each other long enough to figure out they've been tricked, I'll be long gone."

"And the other Apples know what you're up to?"

"They will do whatever I command. You don't think I'd get *my* hands dirty repairing a filthy spacecraft, do you?"

Gavin seemed unconvinced by the plan. "You're sure your parents won't blow up Earth?"

Niki threw her hands up. "This obsession with saving your planet! You need to get a hobby." She put her hands on her hips. "You can be *so* selfish. All you think about is how this affects you. Don't you ever stop to consider other people?"

"You mean the seven and a half billion people on Earth?"

"No." She shot him a withering look. "I mean *me*. Don't worry about your precious Earth – honestly, it's not worth wasting the firepower."

"Niki, promise me. Please."

She sighed. "If it will put an end to your frankly weird sentimental attachment to a four-and-a half-billion-year-old rock." She put a hand over each of her hearts. "I swear not to let my parents annihilate, conquer or otherwise harm this planet and its inhabitants. Happy?"

With Gavin apparently satisfied, she left him to seek out the others. There was much to do before her parents' arrival, and she needed to make a start delegating the more unpleasant tasks to the rest of the Apples.

◆

Given her disdain for all things earthling, over the following days Niki was surprised at the ease with which she settled back into her Middling life. Not that she would ever confess it to the others, and especially not to Gavin, but the moment the car had turned into Park Street and she'd caught sight of their house again she'd experienced a spike of – and there was no other way to describe it – happiness. The next week back at school also brought with it odd, uncomfortable feelings of satisfaction and even stirrings of ... *enjoyment*? First, the student council chose her proposal for the redesigned school badge, and she hadn't even been forced to use her mind-power on anyone to influence the decision. But the main topic of conversation surrounded the freakish weather assaulting the earth. The Galactic League's hot hail attack had merely been the first salvo; more had followed. Every news outlet was buzzing with reports from across the world of unusually violent storms, earthquakes in countries not known for seismic activity, and a very peculiar rain of toads. The last would've been bad enough on the warty face of it, but the toads could also talk. And all they croaked were insults.

"That's definitely my dad's idea," she'd confided to Gavin during one tedious English class. "He thinks he's so funny."

"Yeah, classic dad joke," Gavin had replied with what Niki had come to learn as typical earthling sarcasm.

Across the wider world there was an atmosphere of unease that reached to the furthest corners of the planet. Commentators couldn't agree on a single reason for the strange phenomena, but they did agree that it couldn't bode well. Only Niki, Gavin and the Apples knew that the attacks were the warm-up for an invasion. An invasion that Niki had stalled. For now.

One morning shortly after that she entered Mr Al-Khwarizmi's maths classroom to squeals of what at first she took to be horror at yet another of their teacher's tortuous algebra problems. But she was wrong. A gaggle of her classmates surrounded Tanisha Day, who was clutching the object of their excitement, an ink-based image generated by light falling on an electronic image sensor printed on chemically processed cellulose derived from tree matter.

"It's a signed photograph," Tanisha explained to a baffled Niki.

The image that had provoked such fervour was of Hal Hill and the rest of the band members of Cubic Parsec. It seemed that the previous evening Tanisha's older sister had taken her to the latest concert on their tour, where not only had she acquired the photograph, but also a T-shirt and a mild throat infection. At first Niki couldn't understand the excitement, but as she lingered she felt a strange sensation creeping over her. "Your feeling of elation," she observed. "It is infectious."

"Do you want to hold it?" Tanisha croaked, offering her the photograph.

Niki could see no reason why she should, but she felt compelled to acknowledge her classmate's gesture.

"His eyes!" cooed Tanisha.

195

"His hair!" swooned Audrey Woods.

"Yes," said Niki, nodding in puzzled agreement. "He has both eyes and hair."

At the end of the school day, she and Gavin once again joined the rest of the Apples at number forty-six. They had been hard at work readying the house for its new occupants. Sam had taken a trip to Ikea and picked up a load of furniture, then spent the next three days shouting at it. Bart had set to work cleaning the house from top to bottom, which he viewed as a great workout. Mercedes had been toiling in the garden, planting a colourful but low-maintenance border, and raising the height of the perimeter fence to minimise the risk of D'Rek the Destroyer and Pamnatakrocula the Pitiless's inevitably weird behaviour being overlooked by the neighbours. Gavin had compiled a guide to Middling to help the new arrivals fit in, which included bus routes, a list of local restaurants and a detailed set of instructions on how to interact with the local human population. Niki's contribution was less hands-on. She was a princess, after all.

She dumped her schoolbag on the kitchen worktop, next to Sunshine Starburst, who was perched there apparently in deep conversation with the microwave. Gavin and the Apples continued to fuss in the kitchen,

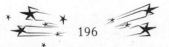

while Bart bustled in the hallway pushing the vacuum cleaner around like it was a rowing machine. Niki drew up a chair and over the drone of the vacuum announced, "I have decided to move in with my real parents for the duration of the challenge. Living in close proximity I will be better able to provoke their mutual animosity."

"Is that a wise tactic, Princess?" asked Mercedes doubtfully.

She and Sam joined her around the newly installed Nordviken extendable table in white to vent their concerns.

"As your guardian," said Sam, "I cannot allow you to be alone with those two monsters."

Niki studied his soulful eyes set deep in his craggy face. The Leontine had been assigned to what the Honour Guard referred to as "princess duty" when she was barely out of her birthing pod. Although the position was regarded as a soft option for a soldier like him, he had taken to his duties with surprising enthusiasm. As well as protecting her, he was responsible for training her in martial arts and strategy. Wherever she went, he was never far behind, usually carrying a selection of edged weapons. When she thought about it, the doughty warrior had been around her during her childhood a great deal more often than her parents. As she grew, she

learned that as a high-ranking member of the Honour Guard he was not permitted to have a family of his own. Once, during a particularly fierce bout of fencing practice, she'd asked him if he wanted offspring. He had answered her between a lunge and parry, and his reply had stuck with her all these years: "I have you, Princess. And you're enough for anyone."

"And what if you need us in an emergency?" said Mercedes, her question jolting Niki out of her recollection.

Mercedes was a relatively new addition to her court. Sam had recruited her only when he decided to flee the League with Niki. The android was programmed to intervene in the princess's medical issues, but it was obvious that Mercedes' concern went beyond a grazed knee or even a broken arm. Was her synthetic brain capable of genuine emotion? Because that's what Niki was detecting now. It was as if her guardians really cared about her. How odd.

A terrible screeching noise made them all flinch. Sitting on the kitchen worktop, Cupcake ran its claws down the tiled splashback.

"I just grouted that," tutted Sam.

"As much as it pains me to agree with the Leontine," said the bounty hunter, "he's right. You can't trust your

parents." The cat shot a look at Niki. "I mean, your mother *invented* the double-cross with a half-reverse betrayal."

"Then you should move in too," said Gavin. "That way if Niki's parents try anything, you'll be right there."

Ever since Gavin had returned for Cupcake aboard Vorlon's ship, the bounty hunter had pledged itself to his service.

"Agreed," said Cupcake.

"Very well," said Niki. "And while we are antagonising my parents, the rest of you will commence repairs on the ship."

Sam continued to voice his objections, but in the end he had no option but to concede to Niki's way of doing things. "Since spaceship parts are not easy to come by in Middling," he said, "we will scour the country and, if necessary, the planet for the vital components. Starburst and I will head off immediately."

The unicorn held up both hooves. "Whoa, whoa, whoa! Not so fast, lion-man." Its horn began to light up frantically. "Will the trip involve staying in any abandoned asylums or passing through quaint villages where all the children have glowing eyes?"

"Not intentionally," said Sam.

Following some more gentle persuasion, Sunshine

Starburst reluctantly agreed to accompany him on the trip. The Leontine warrior and the unicorn AI departed that night. Now all that remained was to wait for Niki's parents to arrive.

Middling had no idea what was about to hit it.

Chapter 23

While Niki and the others finished preparing the house, the Skerlon and Zenobian fleets were held in orbit like a pack of straining attack dogs on a short leash. D'Rek the Destroyer and Pamnatakrocula the Pitiless had reluctantly obeyed their daughter's order not to fill the downtime by conquering Earth, though they'd protested in the strongest terms. What was the point of having an invasion fleet and not using it to annihilate an unsuspecting civilisation? It was unnatural. However, Niki hadn't ruled out fighting each other. So far the casualty count stood at three light cruisers, two heavy cruisers, a frigate, eight fighters and an old Russian TV

satellite belonging to a channel that broadcast round-the-clock opera.

The conflict only paused when, at last, moving-in day arrived. To avoid attracting unwanted attention from the neighbours, two ships in full stealth mode dropped into the atmosphere and navigated to a prearranged rendezvous point outside Middling, far from curious eyes. With Sam and Sunshine off on their mission to acquire spare parts, the plan had been for Mercedes to pick the rulers of the galaxy up in the car and drive back into town, but that had been rejected by both parties. They may have consented to living under the same roof, but they'd nitpicked every other suggestion that might bring them within each other's orbit. They categorically would not share the back seat of a Volvo. In the end, Mercedes returned with D'Rek the Destroyer, and Pamnatakrocula the Pitiless showed up a few minutes later in an Uber.

Waiting on the doorstep of the freshly painted and decorated house at number forty-six, Gavin, Cupcake, the Apples and the lately arrived D'Rek the Destroyer watched her get out of the car.

"Someone else didn't get the memo about being inconspicuous," remarked Cupcake.

She was dressed in a golden jumpsuit and diamond-

studded boots. Over this ensemble was draped a long diaphanous cloak, the back of which trailed behind her on the ground for several metres. Flanking her were a pair of burly soldiers in black uniforms, a head taller than anyone else, wearing respirator masks and holding futuristic rifles. With them at her side, she proceeded along the drive, trailing a gaggle of small grey humanoid creatures with skinny bodies and moon-faces. Two of them picked up the train of Pamnatakrocula's flowing cloak, while the rest staggered under teetering stacks of her luggage.

D'Rek the Destroyer took one look at the approaching retinue and launched into a fresh objection. Niki tuned him out, already weary of his moaning. He had complained non-stop from the moment he'd arrived, and it was clear he'd rather face any number of eight-headed monsters than be forced to cohabit with his ex-wife. At least he had followed Niki's instructions and brought a single suitcase, unlike her mother. Though, like her, he had shown up wearing his formal Invasion Suit, which consisted of full-length scarlet robes, his blinding chest medallion, a pair of jewel-encrusted silver gauntlets and a giant, flaming sword.

However, if either of them was expecting to continue living like a galactic overlord, they were in for a shock.

They crowded into the small front room and Niki clapped for silence before addressing her parents. "No special forces; no slaves," she insisted. "The deal was just the two of you living together like a normal Earth couple."

Pamnatakrocula the Pitiless looked puzzled. "Earthlings have no slaves?"

"Nope," said Niki.

"Then who do they hurl into their Neverending Pit to be feasted upon by their Eternal Shadowbeast?"

"They don't have a Shadowbeast."

The moon-faced slaves perked up at this, oohing and aahing in wonder.

"Silence!" their mistress hissed at them, but it was clear she was unsettled by this revelation.

"You have to send them all away," said Niki.

"Can't I keep just one commando?"

Niki shook her head firmly and her mother conceded with a huff. "Fine."

D'Rek the Destroyer chuckled at her displeasure.

"Don't think I've forgotten about you," said Niki. "No weapons. That was part of the deal."

"But I haven't been unarmed since the day I was born," he complained. "And even then I had my vestigial tail-spikes."

"Weapons. Now." Extending a hand, she waggled her fingers. "And that means *all* of them."

Grumbling, he handed over his flaming sword and fished out a series of guns, grenades and various other deadly-looking alien weapons from the folds of his robes and several secret compartments in his luggage.

"Now we can begin," said Niki. "At the end of one month, I will judge which of you has been the better parent – and will go willingly with him or her."

Her parents glowed with anticipation, then they caught one another's eye and loathing clouded their faces.

Gavin watched in silence from the edge of the room, marvelling at what had become of his life over the last few weeks. Not only had he discovered that his next-door neighbours were aliens, but now two more had moved into the street. Currently, they had more aliens in the neighbourhood than bin collections.

"The first thing you'll need are new names to help you blend in," said Niki.

Gavin knew from her earlier briefing that it was important that the rulers of the galaxy not draw undue attention to themselves, since no one wanted the Earth authorities showing up and making a fuss. If anyone tried to arrest her mum or dad, Niki said they were likely

to unleash a full-scale invasion.

"Since we made a few easily avoidable mistakes when choosing our names, I've consulted our resident earthling." Niki threw out an arm to indicate Gavin.

Her parents, their slaves and bodyguards looked all over the room in confusion.

"Hello. Right here." He waved a hand. "So, names—"

"What's wrong with D'Rek the Destroyer?" said her dad.

"Nothing. It's … um … lovely. Very evocative; just not very Middling. So I was thinking, for you … Derek." He turned to Pamnatakrocula the Pitiless. "And Pam."

"Happy with those?" asked Niki.

They hid their displeasure behind forced smiles. "Of course, hatchling," said her mother, going in for an awkward hug.

Niki recoiled, as much in surprise as anything else. "What are you doing?"

"I have been studying Earth mothers and have observed how they exhibit affection for their offspring." She pinched Niki's cheek hard between bony fingers, saying in a flat voice, "Cutie. Pie."

"I must object in the strongest terms," Derek piped up. "By taking this action you have contravened our agreement." He produced a tablet-like device, the screen

filled with alien type. "As per Section 12, Subsection B, paragraph two, I negotiated the first daughterly embrace."

As the two of them argued over the fine details of their agreement, Niki signalled to the others and they sneaked out of the room to convene in the hallway.

"I think it's going very well," said Niki.

Cupcake gave a disbelieving grunt. "I've been in friendlier bar fights."

Niki ignored it. "I have to collect my stuff from home so I can move in with them. And then the task can officially begin."

"Bart and I will remain here to assist your parents in settling in," volunteered Mercedes. "I still have the bedroom drawers to assemble."

"Didn't Sam already put together all the flat-pack furniture before he went?" asked Gavin.

"It transpires that he's great with a rapid-fire flux disintegrator rifle," Mercedes replied. "But not so much with an Allen key."

She and Bart headed towards the bedroom at the back of the house, to attack the drawers.

"And, Bart," Niki called after him. "Don't let either of my parents persuade you to give them *any* of your major organs. They don't need them, and they'll only be doing

207

it for a laugh."

"Got it! No accidental organ donation." He stuck two thumbs up and disappeared off down the hallway.

"I'll make sure everything stays inside," said Cupcake, padding after him.

"Walk you back to yours?" Gavin said to Niki.

They left the house and the sounds of her arguing parents faded. Niki put her hands on her hips and aimed a satisfied look back at the window where she could see them continuing their hostilities.

"Before this month is up, I will be a thousand light-years away from them – and this planet."

"Yeah, great," said Gavin.

"Isn't it?" she beamed.

Briefly, he considered telling her about his own unplanned departure from Middling, but rejected the idea. She didn't care what happened to him. Not that it mattered. Niki and he would both soon be leaving Middling: her on a spaceship and him in the back of a social worker's car.

Chapter 24

As the only resident human being in the group, Gavin was encouraged to help the newcomers settle into their Middling existence. So it was that the day after the rulers of the galaxy moved into number forty-six, he found himself alongside Niki in the kitchen, instructing Pam and Derek in the practicalities of their temporary new life.

"Earthling, does this activate the perimeter defences?" asked Pam.

"That's the kettle," Gavin explained. "You use it to boil water."

"Ah." She picked it up and tipped the spout. "For

pouring over your enemies as they attempt to scale the walls of your fortress. Primitive, but effective."

"Or," he said, reaching into a box for a teabag, "you could use it for making tea."

"It's an Earth delicacy," Niki added helpfully.

Before Gavin could stop him, Derek had swiped the bag and popped it into his mouth. He chewed a few times and then there was a gulp as he swallowed it down.

"Not bad," he declared.

Pam's voice echoed across the kitchen. "I have found the ice-prison."

Gavin looked over to find her with her head stuck in the fridge.

"It is not very cold," she complained.

"Remember the ice-prison we had on Gorgaro Prime?" Derek said with a faraway look. "We froze six Gorgaron generals in there until they gave up the launch codes."

"And we could've fitted in six more!" reminisced Pam. She closed the door with a fond sigh. She had entirely misunderstood the purpose of the refrigerator, but in doing so revealed one thing. There was no food in the house.

"OK," said Gavin. "We have our first Earth … um … *mission*. We're going to a supermarket."

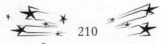

Derek perked up. "Ooh, is that where you purchase your superweapons?"

He and Niki met up with them in the hallway an hour and a half later. It took that long for the two of them to get ready without their usual complement of servants to help. As with their change of names, they had been persuaded to swap their alien regalia for more inconspicuous outfits. Derek arrived first, wearing a tracksuit in the red and white colours of the local football team, Middling United. The one thing he hadn't ditched was his gold medallion. It lay sprawled on his chest, blinding anyone who had the misfortune to look at it directly.

"I am ready to leave the habitation," he said. "You may lower the defensive shields."

Gavin sent a puzzled glance at Niki, who just shrugged. It wasn't worth arguing.

"Uh, OK," said Gavin, lifting his phone and randomly tapping the screen. "Mmmmmmmm."

"Earthling, are you humming like a shield wall?"

"No," he lied.

Pam strutted into the hallway closely shadowed by Cupcake. She had found the closest Earth approximation to her overlord outfit and was wearing a black jumpsuit and high leather boots. Like Derek, she had retained her jewellery – a pair of shrunken planet earrings dangled

either side of her narrow head.

"I have consulted your house AI," she began.

"She means Alexa," explained Cupcake.

"This supermarket, it is for the provision of supplies. *Groceries.*" She spat the word as if it had a bad taste.

"Remarkable," said Derek.

They both seemed unduly surprised at the prospect of visiting the store. "How do you get groceries on your world?" asked Gavin.

Derek waved a hand. "I despatch a task force to invade the planet next door, wipe out their ruling class, subjugate their people and pillage their world for supplies."

It seemed like a lot of effort to go to for a frozen pizza.

"Where's Bart?" asked Gavin, suddenly aware that he hadn't seen him for a while. Pam and Derek responded with blank looks.

"He means my emergency organ supply," Niki explained.

"Ohhh," said Derek, displaying a deep level of uninterest. "That thing."

"*He* is not a thing," she corrected him.

Gavin was taken aback. Usually Niki was as dismissive of Bart as her parents. This was a new side to her, one that for the most part she had kept well hidden beneath an exterior of haughty disdain.

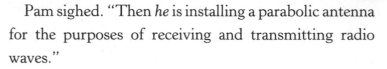

Pam sighed. "Then *he* is installing a parabolic antenna for the purposes of receiving and transmitting radio waves."

Now it was Gavin's turn to stare blankly at them.

"She means a satellite dish," said Cupcake.

"If I have to be stuck here for an entire month," said Derek, "I'm not missing the new season of *Decluttering Your Solar System with Dopkop Zomsin*."

"Oh yes," enthused Pam. "Did you see the one where she tidied the Eddoth and their annoying planet into a black hole?"

Gavin was horrified. "That's terrible."

Pam and Derek regarded him with baffled looks. "Its orbit was displeasingly irregular," said Derek. "It had to go."

"Most therapeutic," added Pam.

Retrieving Bart from a precarious perch on the roof, and with Cupcake left behind to "guard the habitation", they took the bus to the supermarket. At first both of Niki's parents refused to entertain the idea of public transport, insisting that it would demean their high status, but then Gavin informed them that there was a special priority lane reserved only for buses, and Niki added that from the top deck of the double-decker you got to look down on everyone. That was enough to get

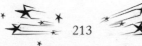

them aboard the 55.

Twenty minutes later they got out at the stop outside the supermarket. Bart strolled inside, declaring that he needed to stock up on chia seeds and lentils, while Gavin paused to grab a trolley.

"I see you have enslaved this species and placed it in servitude," said Pam, admiring the line of chained shopping trolleys. "Well done."

He was about to correct her misapprehension about the trolleys when she asked him, "What do we do now, little cuddle bear?"

"What did you call me?"

"I am practising my Earth terms of endearment," said Pam. "I have memorised seventy-two discrete examples. Is this one not appropriate? Would you prefer some other designation – perhaps 'fuzzy bunny', or '*Honigkuchenpferd*'?"

Gavin was about to ask what that meant but then he noticed Derek, who had wandered into the store and was in animated conversation with a bemused security guard. "Niki!" he hissed, drawing her attention to what was at the very least problematic and potentially a catastrophe.

"Oh no…" she muttered, dashing inside.

Gavin swiftly pushed the trolley after her, skidding to a stop beside the two men. Derek was in the midst of

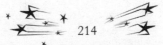

quizzing the guard.

"Plasma disruptor? Meson cannon? Not even a pain-stick?"

The guard drew himself up, trying to maintain a measure of professional courtesy. "As I've already said, sir, it is company policy not to arm its store security personnel."

"Ah, now I understand," said Derek. "You are trained in the deadly art of Aldebaran Karate. A practitioner of that needs no weapon other than his hands, teeth and tail!" Crouching into a ready pose, Derek bared his teeth and emitted a low growl. Then, whipping his hands and arms through the air he challenged the guard. "Let's see how well your brood-mother has trained you."

The security guard was an overweight middle-aged man in a uniform at least one size too small for him, and nothing in his life had prepared him for this encounter. Brass buttons strained across his generous belly as he backed away. Derek took that as an invitation to set off in pursuit and proceeded to chase him around a special offer on Quality Street, knocking over the towering tins with wild chops and kicks. The security guard tripped and fell flat on his well-padded stomach. Derek was about to leap on him to finish him off when Pam called across the store.

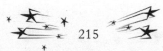 215

"D'Rek, look here at this exhibit."

He broke off mid-pounce, immediately losing interest in the guard and wandering over to Pam in the fruit and vegetable aisle, where she perused the produce as if she was at an art gallery.

Leaving Niki to offer her apologies to the stricken security man, Gavin hurried after her parents.

"Be careful, they may be in their poisonous phase," warned Derek on seeing his ex-wife leaning in to inspect the shelves.

"They're strawberries," said Gavin.

"Never trust any species that wears its seeds on the outside," cautioned Derek.

"D'Rek, do you remember?" said Pam with a wistful air.

He did. Apparently, the strawberries reminded them of the first alien race they had conquered after they were married. For a moment Gavin was sure that he'd caught the two of them gazing fondly into one another's eyes at the memory. But then Niki arrived, and it was as if steel shutters came down between them. They resumed their mutual wary dislike.

"AAAAAH-CHOOO!" Derek let loose a roof-raising sneeze. It was so loud that other shoppers in the supermarket stopped in their tracks, and from two aisles

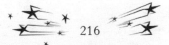

along came the splinter of breaking glass.

"Maybe you're allergic to strawberries," Gavin suggested.

"It's not the strawberries. It's her." He gestured to Pam, his face going into spasm as he built up to another sneeze.

"I emit a natural pheromone to which he is allergic," she said proudly.

"Imagine discovering that on the night of your bonding ceremony," he muttered, unleashing another shuddering sneeze. From another aisle came a second crash as yet more produce hit the floor. "She doesn't have to emit, you know. Can turn it off and on like that." He snapped his fingers.

"Yes," she purred, "but it makes you so delightfully *furious*."

For the next ten minutes the shopping expedition proceeded normally. Pam and Derek sniffed pineapples and squeezed avocados, and Derek declared lettuce part of the Zenobian empire. So, as normal as could be expected. While arguing over pasta, Gavin and Niki briefly lost track of her parents. They found Derek two aisles over surrounded by a thick carpet of cornflakes. They crunched underfoot as he pulled cereal boxes off the shelves, ripping them open and ruthlessly discarding

their contents. Derek glanced up from an empty packet with a puzzled frown. "Where's the Proton Pistol?"

"They don't have free gifts in them any more," said Gavin.

Derek tossed away the packet and reached for another. Other shoppers passing along the aisle were noticing his odd behaviour.

"He's drawing too much attention," hissed Niki. "You need to distract him."

"Me?" Gavin was about to object when he remembered something that ought to grab his interest. "I'm reading your book," he blurted.

Derek dropped the cereal packet instantly. "You are?"

"Oh yes."

The galactic tyrant spun a hand. "A-a-and?"

"I'm at the bit about your great love –" He paused. "– Of immensely powerful weaponry."

Derek steepled his hands and placed them thoughtfully beneath his chin, affecting a look of immeasurable satisfaction.

"*Chapter Eighteen – Who Moved My High-Power Proton Zapper?*" he began, quoting himself. "*Augmented Anti-Matter Phaser. Armageddon Gravity Pistol. I love weapons, the more destructive the better. I even wanted to name my first-born after my favourite Omega Meson*

Ravager, but my partner advised me that it would result in our hatchling being mercilessly teased by her classmates. That was obviously unacceptable – the merciless teasing of my child is reserved only for her mother and me."

He raised his eyebrows at Gavin, clearly expecting some expression of admiration. Not sure what to say, Gavin instead launched into an uncertain round of applause.

"Very … moving?"

Derek beamed at the boy. For someone who had conquered the known galaxy he was remarkably susceptible to a modest amount of praise.

"Speaking of my mother, where *is* Pam?" asked Niki.

No sooner had she spoken than there came a scream from the next aisle and the unmistakable thud of a body hitting the floor.

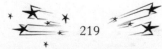

Chapter 25

They bolted round the corner to discover Pam standing astride a middle-aged woman lying in a pool of suspicious red liquid.

Gavin winced. "Blood?"

"Tuscan tomato and basil," said Niki, crouching down and pointing to the label on a smashed jar of pasta sauce.

The woman was sprawled face-down beside her up-ended shopping trolley, its contents spilled across the floor. She moaned in pain.

Gavin rounded on Pam. "What did you do to her?"

"She left me no option."

"I'm really sorry," he said to the fallen shopper, helping her up. "She's from out of town."

"Gavin?" The woman met his gaze.

Oh no. It was Mrs Walker, their neighbour. She and her husband played bridge with Mercedes and Sam every Thursday, believing them to be normal people and not a robot and a Leontine warrior. Brushing herself down, she cast a cautious eye over Pam and Derek.

"Do you know these people?"

"Umm, they're … my uncle and aunt," said Niki quickly. "Uncle Derek, Aunty Pam, this is Mrs Walker."

"Barbara," said Mrs Walker, pointedly ignoring Pam and extending a hand in greeting to Derek, who gazed at the hand in confusion.

Gavin urgently mimed at him to shake it and he gave a tiny nod of understanding.

"And *Bar-bara* to you, earthling." He beamed at Gavin proudly.

Still puzzled, Mrs Walker turned to Niki. "How are your mum and dad? We missed them at bridge night this week."

"They've been sick," lied Niki.

"Oh dear," said Mrs Walker.

"Just a few sniffles," she added.

"Sniffles?!" Derek threw Pam in front of him like a

shield. "They must be quarantined immediately. An unknown pathogen from this planet could do untold damage to my physiological integrity."

Mrs Walker leaned across to Gavin. "Where did you say they were from, dear?"

"Might've known it'd be you lot again," barked a familiar voice. It was the portly security guard. With a weary sigh he surveyed the mess on the floor and pulled at the walkie-talkie clipped to his waistband. "Bravo Two Zero to Control, another glass breakage. Aisle seven."

"He has alerted surveillance units to our presence," scowled Pam. "If they comply with accepted military strategy they will follow up with drone missiles." She lifted her head to scan for the expected strike.

"I beg your pardon?" said Mrs Walker.

"Then beg," said Pam.

A moment later a voice over the supermarket tannoy boomed, "Clean-up on aisle seven."

"Hear that?" cried Derek. "They propose to wipe us out!"

"Wipe *up*," Gavin corrected him.

"Sir, madam, I'm going to have to ask you to leave the store," said the guard.

They ignored him, focused as they were on the anticipated missile strike. When they didn't answer he sniffed, squared his shoulders and uttered the fateful words, "You two, I said hop it!"

"Oh no," Niki mumbled. "If there's one thing you don't do to a pair of megalomaniac rulers of the galaxy, it's order them about."

Pam took a stride towards the guard, so close that he had to tilt his head back to meet her glowering gaze. "You dare speak to *me* like that? I who quashed the Zid uprising, laid waste to the Tarken hordes and toppled the impregnable fortress of Chorwirrn's World?" She grabbed him by the lapels of his uniform jacket and lifted him up as easily as if she were plucking a jar of bolognaise from a shelf.

"Oi, madam!" he said, legs kicking uselessly. "Put me down immediately!"

Out of the corner of his eye Gavin saw Derek's hand dip into a pocket and whip out a device no bigger than a mobile phone. But the detail that alarmed him was what looked suspiciously like a trigger.

"I thought you took all his weapons," he said to Niki.
"So did I."

"Prepare to watch your insides shoot out of your orifices," Derek snarled, levelling the device at the guard. "All of them."

"That's not good," said Niki, as the weapon gleamed

under the supermarket lights. "It's a Molecular Agitator."

Derek squeezed the trigger just as Niki dived at him, knocking him sideways and spoiling his aim. A spiralling red beam shot out of the weapon, raking along shelves filled with jars of pasta sauce. The glass jars glowed red-hot and began to vibrate, clinking against each other so that the air was suddenly filled with a high-pitched ringing.

"What's going on?" The security guard gaped. "What did you do?"

The contents of the first bottle bubbled up and its lid popped off.

"Out," commanded Niki. "Evacuate the store."

Mrs Walker looked at Gavin in confusion. "I would do as she says," he urged.

With a brisk nod, Mrs Walker abandoned her shopping trolley and bolted off down the aisle.

Along the shelf, lids flew off bottles and super-heated sauces fountained over the sides. The molecular agitator caused the volume to double in exponential leaps. Lethal sauces flowed into the aisle without stopping.

Pam lowered the guard to the floor. As soon as his shiny shoes hit the linoleum, he scarpered, pressing the walkie-talkie to his lips. "Emergency Code Ninety-

Nine! Ninety-Nine – yes! The entire store! RIGHT NOW!"

"Yes, earthling, run," Pam called smugly after him. "Run and tell your masters that the Skerlon Overlord has dominion over this Tesco now."

"Not a chance!" Derek objected. "I claim it for the Zenobian Reach!"

Bolognaise, carbonara, pesto and amatriciana flowed like molten lava. Niki and Gavin ran ahead of the spreading sauces, yelling at people to flee for their lives. As they herded the other shoppers to the exit, a whine of static stabbed across the store, as if someone in a hurry was fumbling for a microphone. A new tannoy announcement boomed out. The voice was losing its cool. "Would all shoppers please leave the store immediately. I repeat, leave the store right away! Abandon ship!"

Derek gleefully waved the Molecular Agitator, strafing the shelves on either side of him. Every bottle was blowing its top and the force of the explosions was making everything worse. The shelves rocked to and fro, until they reached a tipping point and fell over, crashing against those in adjacent aisles, creating a domino effect that rippled out across the store. At that point the lake of sauce reached the electrics. The overhead lights began to flicker and pop, and the aroma of garlic was overpowering. Screaming shoppers abandoned their trolleys and fled the encroaching sauce-pocalypse.

At the exit, the security guard shepherded people safely out of the store. Bart appeared from among the escaping shoppers, clutching a basket filled with health foods and a single incongruous packet of salt and vinegar Chipsticks. He looked at Niki with a thoughtful expression. "Y'know, I think someone might be using a Molecular Agitator."

"No kidding," she said. "C'mon. This way."

She and Bart ran past Gavin, shouting at him to get out. He made to follow them, but stopped when he saw Derek and Pam pause next to a display of freshly cut flowers. They were surveying the destruction they'd caused, their eyes shining with vicious delight. The soft drinks aisle went up with a series of fizzing booms, and as the overhead lights sparked like fireworks, Gavin watched Derek reach for the largest and most colourful bouquet of tulips. With one swipe he ripped off the flower heads and offered the bunch of stalks to Pam. She took them, crammed the bare stalks into her mouth and began to chew. The two of them stood amid the devastation, gazing into one another's eyes.

Chapter 26

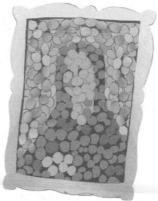

"No way," Niki said flatly. "You must be mistaken."

Gavin had waited until they'd returned Pam and Derek safely to number forty-six (and signed them up to a home delivery app, with express instructions not to atomise the delivery driver) before telling Niki what he'd seen as they fled the supermarket. They were in the hallway when he informed her of the tender moment Pam and Derek had shared, only for her to emphatically reject his version of events.

"Your understanding of our sophisticated extraterrestrial behaviour is primitive. I mean, you're the planet that thought a good idea for a greeting would

be to *shake hands!*"

Honestly, why did he put up with her? "Fine," he said, folding his arms. "I'm just a grunting caveman who cannot possibly comprehend your ways, oh, wondrous and annoying one."

"It is possible that Gavin is correct," said Bart tentatively.

Niki's plan relied on her parents being at each other's throats, not presenting each other with bouquets. "Two beings as evil as those two don't fight each other for control of the galaxy, only to make up over a bunch of carnations."

"Tulips," Gavin corrected her. She glowered at him. "Not important," he mumbled.

Cupcake swanned into the hallway. "You're back. Did you get my smoked salmon?"

Niki ignored the question and stormed upstairs to her room. She needed space to think.

"What about my cheese puffs?" the bounty hunter called after her, before turning to Gavin. "What's up with her?"

"You mean apart from being a stuck-up princess who always thinks she's right?"

He followed Niki, leaving Cupcake below moaning to Bart about its unfulfilled shopping list. Gavin caught up with Niki on the small landing outside her bedroom. Music was coming from the other side of the closed door.

"It's Cubic Parsec," she said.

"Yeah," said Gavin. It was the most popular song of the moment, at the top of every playlist. "That one's even reached us cave dwellers."

"No." She threw the door wide. "I mean ... it's Cubic Parsec."

He looked past her through the open doorway. In the small, sloped-ceiling bedroom under the eaves was a narrow bed, a hastily assembled chest of drawers and four skinny young men with gaunt, handsome faces. Two played guitars, one banged away at a drum kit squeezed between the back wall and Niki's dressing table, while the fourth member of the band stood at the end of her bed, cupping a microphone to his pillowy lips, murmuring the lyrics to "Energy Efficient Window To My Soul".

"It's Cubic Parsec," repeated Gavin dully, his entire body too stunned to share any of its surprise with his voice. He shut his eyes, waited several seconds and opened them again. The band was still there. Contrary to their published tour schedule – and to any rational world-view – the most famous pop group on the planet was in Middling.

In Niki's bedroom.

"Ah, hatchling, I see you have found my gift."

Niki spun at the sound of her mum's self-satisfied voice. Pam was taking the stairs with long-limbed strides, her leather boots squeaking with every step, as if she was walking on gerbils.

"You did this?" said Niki.

"Of course," smiled Pam. "Isn't this what a loving mother does for her offspring?"

"We should probably talk about boundaries," suggested Niki.

"B-but how?" Gavin stuttered.

Pam gestured to the band. "Their earthling minds were easily manipulated. All I had to do was suggest they abandon the forty thousand fans waiting for them in that stadium, and here they are."

"Pah!" said Derek, just behind his ex-wife and breathless from the effort of climbing the stairs. "I have something for you too, daughter. Something that makes the gift of these pale young men ... well ... *pale*." He reached into his tracksuit and pulled out a familiar hardback book. It was *Ruling the Galaxy – A Guide for the Aspiring Tyrant*. He thrust the book at Niki. "You'll need this when you become Supreme Ruler."

He'd forgotten that he'd already gifted a copy to her on

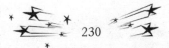

her last hatch-day. And the three before that.

"It's signed. In blood." He flipped enthusiastically to the first page. "Not my own, obviously."

"Great … *Dad*," she said. "I … um … can't wait to read it."

"The *Arcturan Sunday Times* called it 'unputdownable'," said Derek happily.

"You own the *Arcturan Sunday Times*," Pam muttered.

"I own Arcturus," said Derek.

Niki turned to her mum. "And thanks for the … y'know … music, *Mum*."

"It's what all the kids are into right now," she grinned. "At least, according to my interrogation of a representative sample."

"Join us for dinner?" asked Derek.

"We're working our way through your earthling's recommendations," said Pam.

"Happy to help out, Your Majesties," said Gavin.

The two of them jumped at his voice and Derek emitted a high-pitched squeak of alarm. He clutched his heaving chest in fright and addressed Niki. "I wish it wouldn't do that."

Pam shuddered. "These things creep me out. I don't know how you can bear to live among them. Ugh."

Gavin was so used to being overlooked and then

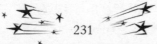

promptly insulted that he'd given up bothering to object to these close encounters of the rude kind.

"Thanks for the invite," said Niki. "But I'm going to Gavin's for pizza tonight."

"Very well." Derek nodded. "Come, my dear." He offered his arm to Pam. "Let us set aside our differences, at least while we sample the Emperor's Feast For Two Including Endless Prawn Crackers. I have a voucher."

Niki watched the two of them descend the staircase and when they were out of earshot she turned to Gavin. "Well?"

"Uh, we're not having pizza tonight."

She flung her arms up. "I don't care about that! Did you see them?"

"More than they saw me."

"They're actually trying to win the parenting challenge. That wasn't part of my plan." She lowered her voice. "I've located their back-up teams."

"But you said no outside assistance. That they had to act like ordinary Earth parents."

She flicked a finger at him. "Is this level of naivety charming to *anyone*?" She sighed at his artlessness. "My parents cheat. That's what they do. Each has landed a ship in Middling containing a unit of the Galactic League's foremost xenobiologists and social studies

graduates."

"Surely someone's going to notice all those aliens."

"Not so. Derek's Chameleon class clipper is using its camouflage tech to pose as a vegan restaurant on the high street. They do an exquisite veggie squash burrito, but you'd better remember to tip the shock troops. And my mother's Deep Space cutter is parked in the outdoor buildings section of the garden centre."

"What's it disguised as?"

"Nothing. It looks like a yurt." She leaned over the banister to double-check that neither parent was listening. "The scientists are advising them on the best strategies to win the parenting challenge. It's possible that they have seen through my ploy, which would explain why they appear to be getting on so well."

"Well, whatever's going on, these alien experts know their stuff. Pam's just kidnapped the most popular band in the world and installed them in your room like a smart speaker."

The last notes of the latest song faded away and the members of Cubic Parsec put down their instruments.

"'Scuse me," said Hal Hill, appearing at Niki's shoulder. His lean handsome face, familiar from a thousand photos, broke into its trademark scoundrel smile. "Me and the boys are going to take a break now.

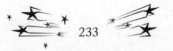

We've been playing for two hours solid."

Niki frowned. "Uh, I don't think so." She fluttered a hand at him. "I have devious plans to adjust, and music helps me think. Back to work, troubadours!"

Hal Hill's smile vanished and his features became passive again. "Yes, Your Highness," he droned, backing away with a low bow. A few seconds later the band launched into "Loft Insulation Blues" and Niki continued to muse on her dilemma.

◆

Despite her best efforts to set Pam and Derek against one another, over the next two weeks her parents grew closer than ever. What's more, they were settling nicely into life on Earth. Pam had started taking a yoga class at the sports centre; Derek had bought a bike and could regularly be seen cycling around the neighbourhood clad in Lycra. They'd acquired library cards and a Netflix account. The two of them were also working their way through Gavin's restaurant guide and tonight they were trying the local Italian trattoria, Leonardo's.

Niki and Gavin spied on them from the pavement outside, noses pressed against the window, listening to accordion music drifting out of the restaurant. Niki cupped her hand to the glass. "Where are they? I can't see them."

"At the table under the painting," said Gavin.

"Is that…?"

"Yup. Leonardo Da Vinci's legendary work of art recreated in salami. They call it the 'Hamona Lisa'."

She squinted at her parents beneath the meat masterpiece. "Do they look happy? I don't think they look happy. I think they look unhappy."

"They're eating the same strand of spaghetti from either end."

"No, look! Pam's getting up. She's going to storm out! Derek's out of his seat too." She frowned. "What are they doing?"

"I think it's called a tarantella."

Her parents were dancing. Oblivious to the rest of the diners, they spun around the dining room to the spiky rhythm of the accordion music.

Niki's face fell. This was not what she'd been hoping for. "It won't last. It *can't*."

Unfortunately, thought Gavin, the way things were shaping up, her plan had the same chance of succeeding as the Hamona Lisa had of being hung in the Louvre. Just two weeks remained until the challenge was up and there was no sign of Sam and Sunshine. They were travelling the country collecting spare parts to repair the spaceship, but they weren't coming back anytime soon,

judging by their weekly reports, which came in the form of postcards.

"Why postcards?" Gavin had asked when the first one arrived, complete with a charming image of the power station at Dungeness.

"My parents will be monitoring all electronic communications," Niki had explained, "so this is the most secure delivery system."

But while Sam and Starburst continued to their search for protective hull coatings, power couplers and all the other bits they needed, there was no ship for Niki to use to escape her parents. Actually, that wasn't strictly true.

"We could hijack the vegan restaurant," Gavin suggested.

"Yes, I briefly considered that option," said Niki, "but it's too heavily guarded. And also it's booked out through the whole of next month."

That left her mum's yurt-craft in the garden centre, but it turned out that the ship had departed after a customer tried to buy it as a centrepiece for their Himalayan garden. So that was that. However, unlike Gavin, Niki remained hopeful about her prospects for outwitting her parents.

"Even if they have reached some kind of truce, it's a fragile one. Last time they split up, each promptly went out and vaporised a solar system. So we just have to find some way of driving a wedge between them. Any ideas?"

There were some experiences that had made an indelible impression on Gavin's young mind. One vivid image swam up from the murk of his past. "Maybe one…"

Niki leaned in closer, a smirk of intrigue plastered across her face. "What kind of twisted scenario are we talking about?"

Chapter 27

"Bowling?" said Niki, screwing up her face in disgust.

Gavin gave a weary sigh. Niki had been doubtful of his plan from the moment he'd laid it out for her a couple of days ago. This was her twenty-third objection. He'd counted.

Mercedes pulled the car through the entrance to Beverly Hills Bowl, a ten-pin bowling and video-game arcade located in a retail park on the edge of town. Surprisingly, it wasn't a knock-off of the Hollywood Bowl; it was owned by a local woman named Beverly Hill. Gavin and Niki had presented the outing to her mum and dad as an activity that regular Earth families

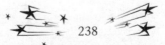

enjoyed and an essential part of their challenge. Whoever won at bowling would edge ahead in the contest. Niki had persuaded Gavin to rope in his nan and grandad too, saying that her mum and dad were more likely to misbehave with an audience. Nan and Grandad hadn't needed much persuasion. It was the first time they'd left the house in ages for anything other than a stroll in the park with the Tiny Horror.

"Are you sure this is going to work?" Niki whispered.

The prospect of waving goodbye to the most maddening person Gavin had ever known remained strong. However, since Pam and Derek had landed in their lives, he realised that in Niki's place he wouldn't want to live with either of those awful people. So, before he too left Middling, he had resolved to do all he could to keep her out of their clutches.

"It's better than your idea," he replied.

She huffed. "Only because of the difficulty of obtaining an aircraft carrier at short notice."

Pam and Derek were already inside, having driven over with Nan and Grandad. Miraculously they'd found a parking space almost immediately. Mercedes, who was driving Niki, Bart, Cupcake and Gavin, had been less fortunate. As one of the few leisure activities available to Middling residents, the bowling alley was hugely popular. Cars had been known to circle for hours waiting for a parking space to open up. Eventually, Mercedes dropped them at the front door and drove off again to continue her hunt. Bart went straight inside and, despite the no pets/bikinis/pets in bikinis rule, Cupcake followed him. Gavin was about to head in too when Niki spoke up.

"Remind me why you believe this will drive my parents apart?"

Recalling an incident involving his previous carers and what was supposed to be a birthday bowling treat, he counted off the reasons on his fingers. "It's horribly competitive, you get to knock stuff down aggressively, eat snacks and drink weird-coloured liquids that give you a massive sugar rush, all in a windowless, music- and sound effect-filled hellish atmosphere. Trust me, by the end of this evening one of your parents is guaranteed to feel sick, defeated and be suffering with a raging headache."

"You're right," she nodded happily. "It's perfect."

The foyer was crammed with people in smooth-soled shoes. Among them Gavin spotted a few kids from school and Bart, marching straight past the shoe-collection counter and vanishing into the crowd.

"Where's he going?" he asked.

"Boogie Boogie Jam Posse," Niki replied.

Bart was heading for the video-game arcade. Boogie Boogie Jam Posse was one of those games where you played by copying increasingly fast and complex dance moves performed by characters on a screen.

"He says it's a great all-round workout." Niki pursed her lips. "But if you ask me, he just loves to boogie."

They found Pam, Derek, Nan and Grandad in a VIP lane. Beyond a swooping set of curtains and a velvet rope were a pair of comfortable couches and a low table set with a candelabra and several bowls of snacks. Grandad was shoving handfuls of Bombay mix into his mouth, while Nan – the Tiny Horror strapped to her chest – told him to take it easy and reminded him about his reflux.

"I didn't book all this," said Niki.

"No, you did not," said Pam gravely.

"I assumed it was an oversight," Derek added. "So I upgraded us for only twenty-nine ninety-nine including bottomless drinks." He held up a colossal paper cup brimming with the frozen delights of a blueberry and strawberry slushie and sucked noisily on a straw for a full minute, before clutching his forehead at what must have been a doozy of a brain freeze. Derek was wearing a garishly multicoloured knitted jumper that was stitched with the phrase "My Invasion Fleet Went to Earth and

All I Got Was This Woven Garment".

"I see you are admiring my choice of apparel," he said with a knowing smile, then reached for a bundle lying on the couch and offered it to Niki. "For you."

It was another jumper, in the same clashing colours, also emblazoned with a slogan. She held it up in front of her. This one read: "Daddy's Little Galactic Princess".

"Isn't it something?!" said Derek enthusiastically.

Niki regarded the jumper in clenched horror. "It's definitely … something."

"Put it on," he encouraged.

With great reluctance, she pulled it over her head. Derek put his arm around her shoulder and drew her close.

"Well, aren't you two just adorable," said Gavin with a smirk, taking out his phone and pointing the camera.

"Don't you dare," Niki hissed. Ignoring her, he fired off half a dozen rapid shots.

Cupcake was also enjoying her discomfort. The bounty hunter spluttered out an amused miaow.

"Oh, look," said Nan. "It's that gorgeous cat that's been following you about, Gavin."

Cupcake preened at the compliment. Grandad made kissy noises while holding out a snack, which it quickly snaffled. The Tiny Horror gurgled and reached longingly

for the cat, so Nan loosened the straps and held the baby close. Promptly, the Tiny Horror stuck its grasping little fingers into the cat's furry neck and Cupcake arched its back in pleasure. Gavin felt a spike of irritation. First the Tiny Horror was taking over his bedroom, now this. Cupcake was *his* cat. OK, his alien bounty hunter.

"Ah, it is detachable!" Pam exclaimed, having watched Nan remove the Tiny Horror from its carrier. "I assumed it was some kind of growth."

Nan's face creased with puzzlement. As far as Nan and Grandad knew, Pam and Derek were Niki's aunt and uncle from "the continent" (though which continent was left purposely unspecified). Gavin and Niki wanted to keep it that way, but statements like that weren't helping.

"Uh, how about we split into teams?" suggested Gavin. "Boys versus girls."

No one was listening. Derek was downing yet another slushie, attempting to get his money's worth out of the upgrade. Meanwhile, Pam had drifted over to the ball dispenser and plucked one for herself. Holding it in one hand, she clenched her free hand into a fist.

"With this mighty projectile I will crush the skulls of my enemies," she crowed.

Gavin glanced at Nan and Grandad. Thankfully,

Grandad was too busy guzzling snacks and Nan had taken the Tiny Horror off to change its nappy. He turned back to Pam. "Uh … that's not… There aren't any enemies, as such."

She reacted as if someone had stolen her puppy. "But I was *promised* skull-crushing."

"That's not how it works," said Niki wearily. Pam's shoulders slumped. "Y'know what, why not let Gavin show you?"

"OK. Yes. Sure." He tried taking the ball from Pam, but she reacted as if he was trying to disarm her. Finally he wrested it from her grip and lined up his shot, before launching the ball down the lane. It rolled straight and true, smacking into the pins and knocking them all down.

"Strike!" he cried. Raising his arms in triumph, he spun round to accept what he was sure would be the hearty congratulations of his fellow players.

They had all gone.

That wasn't quite true. Nan had just returned with the freshly nappied Tiny Horror, and Grandad was reclining on the couch with a bowl of snacks propped on each leg. Neither had noticed his brilliant play. Though that was of less importance than the absence of Pam, Derek and the rest.

"Where did they go?"

"Who?" said Grandad through a mouthful of tortilla chips.

"You mean your friends, dear?" Nan pointed across the alley. "They went that way." He was about to head off when she added, "We had a good chat with Pam and Derek while we were waiting for you."

Uh-oh. Any time Pam and Derek ventured out of the house there was a risk that they'd accidentally expose themselves as alien tyrants.

"Lovely people," Nan beamed.

"They're both in finance," said Grandad, and then he frowned. "At least, I think that's right. Kept talking about hostile takeovers."

Gavin followed Nan's directions, which took him to the video-arcade adjoining the bowling alley. The first thing he saw was Bart, his feet going a hundred miles an hour as he danced his vat-grown heart out while playing Boogie Boogie Jam Posse in front of an admiring crowd.

"Typical," said Cupcake. "You can take the evil galactic overlord out of the planet-annihilator …"

Gavin looked down to see the bounty hunter at his feet. It was gazing across the arcade at another video-game cabinet, its side decorated with an image of a spaceship firing all its weapons and the title "Galaxy Conquest!"

"… but you can't take the planet-annihilator out of

245

the overlord," finished the cat.

Pam and Derek sat side by side in the cabinet, with Niki squeezed between them. In contrast to her scowling face, her parents sported blissful expressions as they wreaked wanton destruction across a virtual galaxy. Gavin hadn't seen them happier since they arrived in Middling.

Niki caught Gavin's eye, extricated herself from the cockpit and marched over.

"So much for your brilliant plan," she complained. *"Bowling."*

"So what do we do now?" he asked.

She shrugged, clearly at a loss.

"Tell me," said Cupcake. "Who would you say is ahead in the parental challenge stakes? Pam definitely gets a point for the pop group in the bedroom, but I would never rule Derek out – when facing certain defeat against the legendary Giant Squidbeast of the Outer Seas, he famously turned the battle around, winning a great victory and a year's supply of calamari. So which one is it? Only, I have a large bet with Bart I'd prefer not to lose."

"What do I care?!" Niki bristled.

"No, really," Cupcake persisted. "Which one of them would you rather spend your life with?"

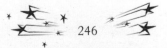

Niki's mouth open and closed. If she was honest, the plan to set her parents against one another had gone awry from the start. Cupcake's question, which she had hoped to avoid answering, now felt real and urgent – like a giant, flaming meteor hurtling towards her out of the atmosphere.

"Maybe it won't be so bad," Gavin said, trying to find a bright side. "I mean, they may be the most merciless rulers the galaxy has ever known, but does that mean they're also bad parents?"

Niki stared straight ahead. "When I was little, they gave me a cuddly toy bear. I named it Mister Bear and took it everywhere with me. When I hugged it, it would make this lovely burbling noise. I loved that bear."

"See," he said. "That's nice."

"I was eight when I discovered the truth." A dark expression clouded her face. "Mister Bear was actually the ambassador from Ursa Major. His name was Auberon and he had a family of his own back on his homeworld. And that cute burbling? His vain attempts to call for help. Then there were my building blocks, fashioned from the bones of their defeated enemies. But Mister Bear and the bones were mild compared with how they came by my trampoline—"

"OK, that's enough!" Gavin didn't want to hear any

more. "Perhaps your mum and dad have changed. I mean, they're really making an effort ... since obliterating the supermarket." Niki threw him a doubtful look. "Fair enough. Come on then, let's get out of here."

"There you are!" It was Mercedes, emerging from the throng in the arcade. "Where are you all going?"

"We're leaving," said Gavin.

She threw up her hands in frustration. "But I just got parked!"

Chapter 28

During her time as a princess of the Galactic League, before Sam and Mercedes spirited her away, a number of courtiers had suggested that Niki's impressive self-belief all too often shaded into arrogance. Not to her face, obviously, since that sort of personal criticism would have resulted in a one-way ticket to a League prison planet. No, these whispers of reproach she had picked up by way of informants and the palace's excellent surveillance technology. It was easy for her to brush off any criticism, believing as she did in her power to shape her own destiny. However, that belief had been tested since Pam and Derek's arrival on Earth. Despite Niki's

conviction that there was no way she would end this month being forced to live with one or other of her awful parents, events over the last few weeks had contrived to make that fate seem all but sealed.

Until last night.

She pedalled urgently along Church Street before swerving through the car park entrance. Gavin followed behind her on his bike, Cupcake perched on the handlebars. Bart jogged alongside them both. They reached the roof level of the multistorey where the broken-down spaceship had lain since its clash with the Gastronite Magicruiser.

The spark and hiss of welding equipment greeted them as they wheeled through the reinstated concealment field. Mercedes knelt on the ship's upper hull, her face behind a protective visor, busily effecting repairs. That was a good sign, but even better was the sight of a dozen or so crates filling the parking bays alongside the ship. The crates were labelled with phrases like "Top Secret" and "Highly Confidential", as well as the logos of a dozen different organisations, ranging from NASA Jet Propulsion Lab and Boeing, to Rolls-Royce and Currys. The spoils of Sam and Sunshine Starburst's mission. They had finally returned from their scavenger hunt, pitching up in Middling late last night when Niki was

asleep. She hadn't seen them then, and they had left by the time she woke up, to commence repairs on the ship first thing that morning. Niki had wanted to duck out of school to help, but Mercedes insisted she maintain the appearance of normality in order not to provoke Pam and Derek's suspicion. As soon as school finished, she and the others had sprinted out of the gates and made their way over.

"Gavin!" Sunshine Starburst cantered down the ship's ramp, leapt into his arms and wrapped its fuzzy arms around his neck. "You have no idea the terrors I was forced to face without you: giant slavering canines, contagion-carrying avians, carnivorous furniture…"

Gavin frowned. "I'm guessing 'big dogs' and 'grotty pigeons', but you've got me with the last one."

"At the northbound services on the M6, Sam lost our petrol money down the back of a Starbucks sofa."

Gavin placed Sunshine back down on the ground. "But you got everything you need, right?"

"Looks like they have enough parts to build a whole new ship," said Cupcake, admiring the numerous crates.

"We're a little short on dynamic dampers," said the unicorn, "but yes, what we couldn't source, we have the components to fabricate."

Niki surveyed the damaged vessel. "Will it be ready

251

by the end of the week?"

Sunshine performed a rapid calculation. "I estimate a seventy-two per cent probability that repairs will be effected before the conclusion of the task you set your parents."

Niki felt a surge of hope. Starburst was the fastest ship in the Galactic League's inventory; at full speed, nothing in either fleet orbiting Earth right now could touch it. For the first time in ages she allowed herself a glimmer of hope – her plan might just work.

"Now, let me tell you about our close call with a vengeful spirit in Cirencester." Sunshine Starburst steered Gavin off, intent on filling him in on the hairy details of its road trip adventure. Cupcake padded after them.

"Bart, go and help Mercedes with the welding," Niki ordered. He set off obediently and she called after him. "Remember to wear your goggles."

He nodded and she caught herself: why was she concerned for her spare part's personal safety? How strange. As Niki contemplated her change of attitude, she became aware of music coming from nearby. She followed the music aboard the spaceship, to find Sam alone in the damaged cockpit.

The effects of the Gastronite attack were evident in

the scorched control console and the tangle of wires that tumbled from broken panels in the bulkhead. Sam was hunched over his electric guitar and singing to himself in a croaky voice. It was a sad song about nothing lasting forever and tryin' to kill the pain, ooh yeah, and the cold November rain. Having been in bed when he returned last night, this was the first time she'd seen him in several weeks. Happiness swept over her, the feeling taking her by surprise. Arching his back, he tipped his head and shook his great mane of frizzy hair, wringing every note of emotion from the song. As the last notes died, he saw her standing there.

"Princess!" A smile split his face and for a moment she was sure he was about to wrap her in a giant hug, which would have been a gross breach of protocol. So why was she disappointed when he stopped himself? Instead, he propped his guitar against the bulkhead.

"Can't fly, but she still has an awesome speaker system."

"Why the sad song?" she asked. "We've a fighting chance to repair the ship and escape in time. That should make you happy."

He swiped the bobble-head figure from the console and flopped down in the forward seat. "That's just it, Your Highness. I'm sad to be leaving Earth. I like living among these people. And I truly believed we could make a life here." He looked at her. "All of us."

Niki felt a guilty pang – after all, it was her broadcast that had led her mum and dad to their front door. Quite literally.

"Are you feeling well?" he asked. "You seem shaken."

"I'm fine," she lied, and pretended to be fascinated by the battle-scarred console. Dented in places and blackened in others, nonetheless it remained partially operational. At that moment a section lit up and an automated voice bleated, "Intruder alert!" An external camera blinked on, displaying an image of the parking bay where a small cylindrical object had burst through the concealment field and was flying towards the ship. Sam sprang into action, grabbing the nearest object to use as a weapon, which happened to be his guitar.

"Stay here, Princess!" he ordered, racing from the cockpit.

Ignoring him, Niki followed him along the gangway and down the ramp. She spotted the flying cylinder immediately. It was the size of a kitchen dustbin, jet black, with no obvious means of propulsion. A pair of dazzling red dots twinkled from halfway up the casing. The others watched it from a distance.

"What is it?" asked Gavin.

"Skerlon attack drone," replied Sam, raising the guitar in readiness.

The drone darted past him, bearing down on the ship.

"Look out!" yelled Mercedes.

There was the flash and whine of pulse weapons as the attack drone laid waste to the crates, blasting their contents so that the precious repair materials were reduced to a series of molten metal puddles. The strike was over in seconds. The drone powered down and settled into a silent hover. There was a faint whirring noise as a small hatch slid open in its top casing and an arm extended. Cupcake aimed its gauntlets and Sam brandished his guitar like a club, ready to take a swipe, but Mercedes stalled them with a raised hand.

"Wait!" she cried. "It's not a weapon."

Warily, the bounty hunter retracted its claws and Sam lowered his guitar. The arm articulated towards the group and the tip lit up, projecting a holographic image of Pam and Derek.

"We bring you greetings from forty-six Park Street, Middling," said Derek.

"First, allow me to applaud your deception, Princess," said Pam.

Niki was suddenly aware of an awkward tingling sensation on her scalp, and it wasn't from her fire-hair.

Pam continued. "I suspected that you would attempt to double-cross us and escape Earth on the Starburst vessel."

"A suspicion confirmed by this." Derek held up what appeared to be a photograph of a large concrete structure, and began to read. "Greetings from Preston Central Bus Station."

It was a postcard from Sam and Sunshine, presumably intercepted by her parents' spy network. Niki muttered a silent curse – she knew they should've gone with carrier pigeons.

"Now you know that we know about your thrillingly duplicitous nature and also that we have stopped your plan before it even got off the ground," said Pam, "I will get to the true purpose of this drone message." She addressed the wider group. "We invite you –"

At this point her voice was replaced by the oddly flat tone of a computer-synthesised voice. It was like one of those form letters where to make it seem personal they shove in your name.

"– treacherous conspirators and human collaborator –"

Pam picked up again from there. "– to a celebration marking a historic moment in our hatchling's life."

"Cheese and wine will be mandatory," added Derek.

"It's not an attack," said Sam. "It's a party."

Its message delivered, the drone retracted its arm, spun round and whizzed off out of the car park, leaving Niki and the others to survey the devastation it had wreaked. Thick braids of smoke swirled from the blasted remains of the equipment and an acrid tang stung the back of Niki's throat. It was the taste of defeat. The drone strike had ended any hopes she clung to of escaping the planet – and her parents. For a moment she felt overwhelmed with sadness, but that was swept away by an altogether more urgent emotion.

Anger surged within her. Anger such as she hadn't felt since her days as a princess of the Galactic League. Back then she had been taught one thing above all else – those with the power are always right. If something went wrong, it was always someone else's fault. Her mum and dad had caused this; they were the source of her misery and frustration. But they weren't here. She rounded on Mercedes and Sam.

"We'll think of something, Princess—" he began.

"Silence!" She cut a hand through the air, her hair igniting with her fury. "You brought me to this planet to get away from my parents, but they're here anyway."

The Apples absorbed her rage in deferential silence, but Gavin was aghast. "You were the one who led them here."

257

His words met her incandescent anger and boiled away into nothing.

"You promised to protect me. But you failed." She continued to berate them, her flame-hair leaping ever higher. "This is all your fault. Not mine. I didn't ask for any of this."

"Niki, what are you saying?" Gavin yelled at her. "Stop it!"

But she didn't want to stop. In fact, it was a relief to unleash this aspect of her nature, something she had been forced to bottle up during her time on Earth. "You're pathetic, all of you. And even if we had run from my parents again, where would we have gone, hmm? You would have dragged me to another mind-numbing world –" She turned her baleful gaze on Gavin – "full of tediously forgettable inhabitants." She could tell that he and the Apples were reeling, but she had one last swipe to deliver. What on Earth they called the *coup de grâce* – the killer blow. "At least if I go with my real mum or dad, I'll be rich and powerful – and I won't have to look at any of your loser faces for one more Galactic minute."

Her tirade over, she let that sink in, and though the eyes of her guardians were turned to the floor she could see their stricken expressions. Only Gavin met her gaze, disappointment and incomprehension etched in his

features. The elation that had powered her anger subsided and she was struck briefly by another, unwelcome feeling. Remorse. She shrugged it off; a galactic princess did not entertain such weakness. This was who she was and no amount of time spent in Middling with these beings could change that. Though what did it matter anyway? Her time here, with all of them, was almost at an end. Niki hardened her heart and marched off.

Chapter 29

For the first time since they had met on the steps of Middling High School, Gavin was the one pursuing Niki. She hadn't been at school all week and when he cornered Bart in maths to ask how she was doing, he just shrugged, saying that he didn't know and, what's more, he didn't care.

"Let it go, kid," said Cupcake after school one day towards the end of the week. They were in what was for now still Gavin's bedroom. Sitting on the edge of the bed he glanced across the floor to where the Tiny Horror lay on its back, gurgling happily, as Cupcake dangled what he hoped was not an alien weapon system above the

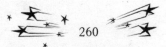

baby's head.

"You'll never understand her. She's galactic royalty – they're different from normal beings like you and me."

Let it go. It was the kind of smart, sensible advice Gavin would've followed in the past. Wherever he'd lived, there was always the occasional kid who'd invite him over to play video games, or at school ask to sit with him at lunch, but he'd always shun them. Making friends was risky when you didn't know how long you were staying in one place. However, with Niki it had been different. She hadn't given him any say in the matter, just blazed into his life and now, whether he liked it or not, he realised that they were friends. Gavin couldn't let it go.

"I'll be back in five minutes. You OK if I leave you two here?"

"Relax, I'll take care of everything," said Cupcake, circling the Tiny Horror, green eyes fixed on its chubby little body. "OK, Tony, time for din-dins." The bounty hunter licked one of its gauntlets and levitated a bottle of formula, which pivoted horizontally and shot into the baby's mouth. "Drink up, kid."

"That's just formula, right?" Gavin asked nervously.

Cupcake threw him an admonishing look.

Gavin slipped out of the house and made his way

along Park Street. In preparation for her departure, Niki had been spending all her time with Pam and Derek at number forty-six. So for the last week he had gone round every day after school intending to talk to her. However, each time he rang the bell Pam or Derek would answer and insist that she wasn't home. Which he knew was a lie. Partly because they would say things like "She's busy with her live firing practice" or "She's just dropping off a parcel on Saturn", but mostly because he could see her at her bedroom window, staring out with big, round eyes and sighing a lot.

He could see here there now, gazing forlornly into the distance. And idly picking her nose. Her window was open, so he called her name and waved his arms above his head, like a shipwrecked sailor trying to attract the attention of a passing plane. But after a full minute of calling out her name and some desperate flapping, during which he was sure she had to have noticed him, Niki tugged at the latch, closing the window with a thud, before retreating swiftly into the shadows of her room.

Disconsolate, Gavin lowered his arms and slunk off back home, knowing that the next opportunity he'd get to talk to her would be the night of her going-away party. It would also be the last.

Gavin lay on his bed in his room, poring over Derek's book. He was hoping to unearth some overlooked detail about the galactic tyrant that might provide him and the Apples with a last-gasp way out of what was becoming an increasingly dire situation. He searched the pages for a hint that Derek and Pam weren't as invulnerable as they seemed. Surely there had to be some kind of weakness that he and the Apples could exploit to turn defeat into victory. But if the galactic tyrant had a kryptonite, he had made a point not to catalogue it in his book. Instead, Gavin was given an insight into what Niki's future would hold. He read the passage with a sinking heart.

✦

When I first set out on my unstoppable quest for galactic power, kids weren't on my radar. I didn't want to be tripping over a pram in the hallway of my Fortress of Chaos. But then I met the being who was to become the dark love of my life. She didn't want kids either, but you've got to have someone to inherit all that power, right? Is being a dad the best thing to happen in my life? No. Not even close. I'm the ruler of the flipping galaxy! But since having a hatchling of my own I've thought of myself less as a ruthless tyrant and more as father to the whole galaxy. And if there's one thing I've learned as Supreme Daddy, it is the importance of making your offspring compete for

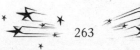

your affection. Keep them at arm's length, withhold your
approval and, above all, never remember their birthday.

◆

The day of the farewell party duly rolled around. The celebration was set for the final night of Pam and Derek's month-long residence on Earth. A fitting end to what had been a surprisingly harmonious stay.

"What you gonna wear?" asked Cupcake, padding about Gavin's feet as he surveyed the contents of his wardrobe.

The invitation came with a dress code, the theme being: *Come as a servile subject at the court of a mighty galactic ruler.* Pam and Derek were a lot of things, but subtle was not one of them. Gavin was in no mood for playing dress-up, so he made a token effort by flinging on a dressing gown with a rocket logo and grabbing a light-up plastic space sword he'd never played with. It had been a present from one of his previous carers, who was obsessed with sci-fi and determined to get him into it too. To the carer's dismay, Gavin showed no interest in laser-swords, alien planets or evil space empires. A position he would have been happy to maintain for the rest of his life, had it not been for the arrival of the Apples. The sword wasn't working, so he replaced the batteries with new ones and thumbed the button on the

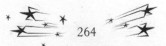

hilt. The plastic blade illuminated a dazzling pink.

"Nothing like making an effort," said Cupcake, casting a sarcastic eye over his costume.

The bounty hunter put on its gauntlets and bandolier and accompanied Gavin downstairs to wait in the hall. Nan, Grandad and the Tiny Horror had also been invited to the party, along with most of the residents of Park Street. As keen as they were for a night out, getting Nan and Grandad to leave the house along with all the paraphernalia required for the Tiny Horror was like mounting a polar expedition. Cupcake sloped off to see if they were nearly ready while Gavin kicked his heels. Bored of fiddling with the light-up sword, he checked his hair in the mirror above the hall table. Still brown. He glanced down at the table and noticed, poking from among a pile of mail, an official-looking envelope from the council. It was addressed to Nan and Grandad but scrawled on the cover in Nan's curly handwriting was the phrase: *Gavin paperwork*. He felt numb. He knew exactly what was inside: the documents that would confirm he was leaving Middling. He was about to slip a finger under the flap when he heard Nan and Grandad entering the hall. Hurriedly, he tucked the envelope into a pocket of his dressing gown.

"What do you think?" asked Nan.

She stood there in a home-made spacesuit constructed from kitchen foil, complete with a mixing-bowl helmet. She'd doctored one of the Tiny Horror's babygrows so that it resembled an alien creature and strapped the baby to the front of her spacesuit in such a way that it appeared to be bursting out of her chest. Next to them Grandad had fashioned an extra pair of arms from cardboard tubes and covered his bobble hat in whatever silver foil Gran hadn't monopolised for her suit. Then he'd stuck three ping-pong balls along the front and painted pupils on them like eyes. All three gazed at him with big, unblinking eyes (and big, unblinking ping-pong balls).

Miserable at the discovery of the council letter, he mumbled that their costumes were nice.

"Shall we go then?" said Grandad brightly.

Gavin deactivated his plastic sword and, tucking it into the cord of his dressing gown, followed them out of the house. He was sure the night couldn't get any worse.

He couldn't have been more wrong.

Chapter 30

The party was in full swing by the time they reached the driveway of number forty-six. The burble of conversation drifted out of the half-open front door along with Pam and Derek's choice of music.

"Calling occupants of interplanetary craft," trilled a lovely female voice.

Grandad paused. "Haven't heard that one since nineteen seventy-six."

They strolled inside and while Nan and Grandad mingled and Cupcake laid siege to the buffet table, Gavin went to find Niki. The house was crammed not only with Park Street neighbours, but also various other

guests including the postman, the lady who ran the flower stall, and the guy who walked up and down the high street wearing a placard announcing The End of the World is Nigh. For a pair of maniacal rulers of the galaxy, Pam and Derek were oddly sociable. The galactic fiends had turned two kitchen chairs into makeshift thrones and placed them at one end of the living room where they were accepting tributes (i.e. presents) from the costumed neighbours, behaving with such solemnity that everyone else clearly thought it was a great joke. They had no idea that Pam and Derek were utterly serious. Derek looked every inch the all-powerful sovereign with his red silk robes and flaming hair. He sat there, noisily gobbling kebabs served to him on a silver tray, while juices dribbled down his chin. Pam, if anything, looked even more scary. Wrapped in a shiny skintight bodysuit she was once more the shadow-mistress and seemed to inhabit her own circle of darkness just in front of the log-effect gas fireplace.

Nearby, Nan cuddled the Tiny Horror, nuzzling its head and making annoying goo-goo noises. She noticed Derek staring and offered him the baby. "Would you like to?"

He raised a hand and gave a loud burp. "I couldn't eat another thing."

Smaller versions of the attack drone that had delivered the party invitation buzzed around the room with platters laden with canapés and various foods impaled on sticks.

"Enjoy," said one of the drones, hovering next to Gavin.

"I'm OK, thanks."

"EN. JOY," the drone insisted, thrusting a tray of sausages on sticks under his nose. Deciding that it would be safer not to argue, he took one and continued scouring the room for Niki. She wasn't there, but he did spot Mercedes and Sam. Niki had said such terrible things to the Apples – unforgiveable things – that Gavin was surprised they'd even shown up to her farewell party. The android and the Leontine warrior sat at a card table in a corner of the room, projecting the kind of glowering air that kept most other partygoers at bay. Gavin sidled into the seat beside them. He hesitated to ask if they'd seen Niki, knowing how things remained between them, so instead he made an inconsequential comment about the party. As banal as it was, it provoked a strong a reaction from both of them.

"I hate this music," Sam announced.

"And what bizarre food combinations," said Mercedes, gagging on what appeared to be a smoked salmon and cream cheese blini.

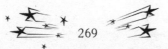

Gavin continued to make awkward small talk and then it struck him that until that moment he hadn't stopped to think what would happen to the rest of the Apples once Niki had gone.

"Are you going to stay in Middling?" he asked.

Sam gave a sour laugh. "As much as I would like to continue playing bridge with the Walkers every Thursday and perfecting the complete works of Guns'N'Roses, in the eyes of D'Rek the Destroyer I have betrayed the Galactic League. My punishment will be to serve out the rest of my life toiling in the Abyss of Souls, mining for diamonds to swell the royal treasury. As for Mercedes, her core systems will be completely erased and she will be repurposed. She will have no memory of any of us."

Mercedes nodded dismally.

"And Bart…" Sam sighed. "For some, he has always been dispensable. Not to us. He remains useful to the princess as spare parts, for now. But he will be replaced soon enough, and then he will be … recycled."

Gavin didn't know what to say – it was all too horrible to contemplate.

"However, the worst fate is reserved for the princess," said Sam. "Her parents will force her to become just like them: the Destroyer or the Pitiless."

"Niki's not like that," Gavin said firmly. "Yes, she's

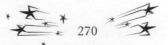

massively annoying, but she's no destroyer. And as for pitiless, never tell her this but I saw her crying when we were watching a film together. Admittedly, it was *Avengers* and it was when Thanos was finally defeated."

"As strong as she is, Pam and Derek are stronger," said Mercedes. "Whoever she chooses, in time they will turn her into the perfect heir to their twisted empire."

Gavin swallowed, and in an attempt to avoid prolonging the awful realisation of their fates, he broke eye contact. It was then he caught sight of a sparkly hoof on the floor beneath the card table. He bent down to see Sunshine Starburst sitting there. The unicorn hadn't noticed him, too intent as it was on studying a multicoloured pastry clasped in one hoof.

"What are you doing?" asked Gavin.

"Ah, Gavin," it said, briefly looking up before returning its gaze to the pastry. "It seems that since inhabiting this body I have developed an inexplicable attraction to rainbow doughnuts. Rainbow anything, actually."

That wasn't terribly helpful. Gavin was about to pull away when Sunshine Starburst added, "And I have been monitoring communications between the orbiting Skerlon and Zenobian ships. A transport shuttle is on course for Middling. Niki and whichever parent she

chooses will leave Earth within the hour."

With such little time remaining, Gavin resumed his search for Niki with greater urgency, only to be immediately assailed by a drone carrying a platter of cheese and pineapple on sticks. In an effort to dodge the machine, he lifted a corner of a white tablecloth and ducked underneath the table.

Bart was already there, sitting cross-legged and silent. His enduring grin had slipped and instead his head was in his hands, face turned to the floor with a hangdog expression.

"Cheese and pineapple attack drone?" asked Gavin.

He shook his head. "Bomb defusal robot with a Greek salad." He looked even more miserable than Sam and Mercedes.

"Are you going to speak to her before she leaves?" Gavin asked.

Bart shrugged. "Can't imagine why. She obviously doesn't want to be with us."

Gavin could hardly argue. In his experience, families didn't stay together however much you wanted them to.

There was a buzzing from above and then the tablecloth flew up, revealing another attack drone carrying a fresh plate of food. It pushed towards them, bleating, "Melon and ham on sticks! Canapés are compulsory!"

The boys fled in opposite directions. Moving through the crowded house, aware that time was rapidly running out, Gavin located Niki at last, hiding out in the kitchen. Like him, she hadn't gone to much effort dressing for the party. It was ironic, he thought, looking around at the glittery-costumed neighbours pretending to be aliens, that a real galactic princess was sitting right in front of them in jeans and a T-shirt, miserably shovelling Pringles into her face.

She paused to look him up and down. "Nice dressing gown – did you steal it from your grandad?"

At least she wasn't still avoiding him, though clearly she hadn't lost her ability to hurl an insult. "Y'know, some people might be pleased at not having to put up with that sort of comment for much longer," he said. "Me, I'm going to miss it."

"Such a simple creature," said Niki.

"Are you really going with them?"

"One of them, yes." She paused. "Unless in that entry-level mind of yours you are harbouring a brilliant last-gasp escape plan?"

"I read your dad's book hoping to find something."

"And?"

He shook his head. "I'm sorry."

"Don't be. Remember, while you toil through another

excruciating English lesson with Mrs Caesar, I get to be ruler of the galaxy."

"I'll take English, thanks."

She raised one eyebrow. "Even if it's Jane Austen?"

"Don't push it."

She grinned, and Gavin realised it was the first time he'd seen her smile in weeks.

"Oh, I'm leaving you a few personal items." She counted them off on her fingers. "My collection of coloured glass dolphins, my mind-wiping toothbrush, Cubic Parsec…"

"Promise me one thing," he said.

"Absolutely not. But ask me anyway."

"Promise you won't end up like them." He didn't need to specify who he was talking about.

She crammed another handful of Pringles into her mouth and gave a non-committal mumble.

"If it's any consolation," he said glumly, "you're not the only one leaving Middling."

"Yes, I heard that Audrey Woods is moving," she remarked. "Strangely anxious girl."

Gavin sighed. "Not her. *Me*." She looked confused, so he explained how the Tiny Horror was getting his room and he'd be moving out.

Niki nodded in apparent understanding. "Is it

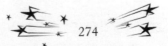

274

because the infant stage of your species is so much more adorable?"

What did he expect? "*I'm* adorable," he muttered.

"Where will you go?" asked Niki. "When you leave here."

Gavin shrugged. "Back into care, I suppose."

Then a thoughtful expression slid across her face and finally she said, "Come with me."

He drew back in surprise. "With you? Into space?"

"We'd only be in space for a while. After that, your days will pass within one or other of the Galactic League's strongholds: the Impregnable Fortress of Chaos or the Immortal Doomsday Bunker. They're a lot like Middling."

"They are?"

"No. Not remotely. But I thought that might make you more comfortable with the idea."

Gavin gazed at the strange alien girl who had lately exploded into his life. To say that her offer was unexpected would have been a wild understatement. Of course he couldn't go with her; people like him didn't move to alien planets. And anyway, after their close call with the Gastronite he'd had enough of space travel for one lifetime. He said he'd think about it, but they both knew what that meant.

From elsewhere in the house came the distinctive ring of a struck gong. "The royal summons," she said, slipping off her chair. She swallowed hard. "Time to choose."

The living room was abuzz with expectant party guests. Gavin and Niki pushed their way to the front, where the other Apples had already gathered. Cupcake was here too, along with Sunshine Starburst, propped on a shelf pretending to be a toy. From their kitchen-chair thrones Pam and Derek and surveyed the assembled party with self-satisfied expressions.

"Hatchling, come here." Pam beckoned to Niki. "Between us."

Grudgingly, she complied. The flying drones lined up behind the thrones and at a signal from Derek they sounded a trumpet fanfare.

"People of Middling," Derek boomed, "this is no ordinary celebration."

"The girl you know as Niki Apple is not who she seems," said Pam.

The Apples exchanged frantic looks. What were Pam and Derek up to? Did they intend to expose Niki as an extraterrestrial?

Derek pulled himself up to his full seated height. "She is, in fact, our daughter."

There were gasps from the party guests. Gavin noticed Nan and Grandad exchange a surprised look. Sam scowled and folded his arms, Mercedes appeared hurt and concerned all at once, and Bart turned away in disgust.

"Tonight marks a significant turning point for our *precious* hatchling," said Pam.

The moment had finally arrived for Niki to make her choice.

"For tonight we give her the greatest gift any offspring could wish for," said Derek.

"We give her … a family," said Pam.

What was going on? Gavin caught Niki's eye. She looked as confused as he felt.

"Yes, hatchling," said Pam. "By inviting us to Middling you have given us what I understand earthlings refer to as a second honeymoon."

"Remember the first?" Derek said to her. "There was you, the moon…"

"And then no moon." Pam gave a fond sigh of remembrance. "My first planetary satellite annihilation."

Derek clasped Pam's hand in his. "Our time together this last month has shown us the truth: there are no two beings in the galaxy more perfectly suited to one another."

277

One the neighbours let out an "aww", believing this to be an extraordinarily romantic declaration, rather than the life sentence that Gavin and the Apples knew it to be.

"What a lovely man," said Grandad, clearly incapable of spotting a tyrannical ruler at ten paces.

"Princess," said Derek. "Your mother and I are officially back together."

Niki looked like she was about to barf.

"Hatchling, I discern from your expression that you know what this means. That, and your agitated brain activity as measured by my attack drones."

Of course. If they were back together then—

"You no longer need to choose between us," said Pam.

"You will come home with *both of us*," said Derek.

Niki's face went white with shock, while all around her the unknowing neighbours greeted this latest development with delight. There had never been anything like it in Middling. The neighbours cheered and applauded. Derek's hair ignited in pleasure, the flames leaping so high that they caught one of the hovering drones, setting it alight and sending it spinning to destruction amid the crowd. The party concluded in smoke and screaming, which seemed entirely appropriate under the circumstances.

The departing guests poured out of the front door,

fleeing the chaos. Gavin, Nan and Grandad were swept along in the noisy exodus and would have been carried along the road, had Gavin not dug in his heels. He stood firm on the pavement outside number forty-six while terrified guests coursed past him on either side.

"Niki's really leaving," he said, looking back at the house. The lights were on in all the windows and he could see Pam and Derek dealing with the blaze in the living room.

"Oh, Gavin, I'm sorry." Nan put an arm round him.

"I'm sure you can stay in touch," said Grandad. "Maybe visit each other. Do you know where they're moving to?"

Gavin muttered something about it being a long way away, but then the Tiny Horror woke up and began to wail. Blasted baby! Maybe it was the crying, maybe it was tiredness, maybe he'd just had enough, but Gavin's hurt at being kicked out to make room for the squalling thing bubbled over. "I know what you're doing," he snapped. "I've seen the letter."

"What letter?" said Nan, at the same time trying to soothe the Tiny Horror.

He fished out the envelope from his dressing-gown pocket. "It's from the council. You're giving the Tiny Hor— the baby my room, aren't you?"

279

Nan looked puzzled. "Well, yes, but—"

"I knew it! I knew you were kicking me out." He felt tears prick his eyes.

"Kicking you out?" Nan sounded distraught.

"Gavin, you don't understand." Grandad took the envelope and extracted a sheaf of documents. "This is planning permission. We're converting the attic into a new bedroom *for you*."

A bedroom.

For him.

"We wanted it to be a surprise," said Grandad.

Mission well and truly accomplished, thought Gavin, reeling from the unexpected revelation. He snatched back the letter – he had to make sure what they were saying was true – but he couldn't read it as the words seemed to be zipping around the page. Somewhere far away he could hear Nan and Grandad's anxious voices asking him if he was all right, if he needed to sit down.

"I thought you were sending me away."

Nan cut him off, wrapping him in a big hug. "Oh, Gavin, if only we'd known you were so worried."

"Sorry, son," said Grandad, joining the embrace. "We should've told you sooner."

Gavin felt a wave of relief. No, waves didn't cover it. Happiness and relief were twin elephants trampling

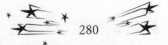

him underfoot. Shock was a wet haddock repeatedly whacking him about the face. How could he have got it so wrong? And yet it had turned out so right. For him, at least. He wasn't leaving. He was staying here with Nan and Grandad. And the Tiny Horror – well, you couldn't have everything. But even in the midst of his tumultuous feelings, his thoughts flew to Niki.

There was a boom from high above in the night sky.

"What was that?" asked Nan with a start.

"Thunder," said Grandad. "Come on, let's get inside before the rain starts."

"You go," said Gavin. "I need to speak to Niki."

"Don't be long," Nan called back as, cradling the Tiny Horror, she and Grandad set off for home.

Gavin stood on the now empty pavement, eyes fixed on the dark clouds overhead.

It wasn't thunder.

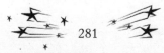

Chapter 31

The Galactic League Lander arrived on silent wings. There was no mucking about with multistorey car parks; on the stroke of midnight the pilot put the craft down in the small back garden of number forty-six. As it touched down, one wingtip knocked over the wall that bordered next door, which the neighbours would only discover in the morning when Dr Aziz left for work promptly at seven forty-five. But by then the ship – and Niki – would be long gone.

Inside the house the drones, which had spent the evening forcing unwanted snacks on people, were now conducting a ruthless clean-up using their built-in

weaponry to disintegrate leftover plastic plates and cups. The air hung heavy with blaster-fire and sadness.

In the living room, Niki stood between her parents, resplendent in their League garments. Derek's crown of fire flickered contentedly, the flames reflected in Pam's dark eyes. Flanking them at either end of the fireplace like a couple of gargoyles lurked a pair of imposing soldiers. They were League troopers; man-sized armoured slugs, their glistening arms holding multi-barrelled assault rifles. Now that the challenge was at an end, Pam and Derek had regained access to the full, terrifying power of their reunited forces. Gavin and the Apples stood on the other side of the room, waiting anxiously.

The door opened and Niki entered. She had changed out of her Earth clothes and was wearing a silver jumpsuit and matching knee-high boots like the ones Pam favoured. Her hair was piled on top of her head in a formal style, finished off with a sparkling tiara. There was a streak of purple make-up around her eyes and her fingernails were painted with shining purple varnish. She looked like a being from another world.

"I am happy to see you properly attired," Pam said admiringly. "Those Earth rags did not befit a princess of the League."

"I have something to say," Niki announced. "It affects

all of you." She turned first to Gavin. "Thanks to the benevolence of the Galactic League and in return for my willingness to accompany my parents, they reaffirm their promise not to destroy the Earth, either out of revenge or spite, or by accident."

Derek stuck up a finger. "Although we can't be a hundred per cent sure about that last one." He shrugged his shoulders. "Sometimes these things happen."

"Thanks?" said Gavin.

Niki held out a backpack to him, its contents jangling as she passed it over. No doubt the promised collection of glass dolphins and weird toothbrush she'd said she was leaving behind. Though presumably not Cubic Parsec, unless they'd been subjected to some kind of shrink-ray. Given the company, it was a real possibility. Nervously, he stole a look inside the bag. There were the glass dolphins, the weird toothbrush, but no miniaturised pop group. Phew.

Niki moved on to the Apples. "You are pardoned for your part in abducting me."

"However, your actions cannot go entirely unpunished," put in Pam. "Daughter?"

The Apples braced themselves for the bad news.

"You are to be exiled," said Niki. "Doomed to live out your lives here on planet Earth."

The frown lines on Sam's wrinkled brow vanished. "What did you say?"

"You get to stay," said Niki. "It's what you wanted, right?"

He paused and then slowly shook his head. "My wish was for the four of us to live here together." He gathered himself, straightening his back and giving a formal neck-bow. "Thank you, Princess."

Mercedes went to hug her, but Niki pulled back.

"Very well," said Pam. "We depart as soon as the Lander pilot has had his sandwiches."

Derek flicked a finger at Bart and issued a command to the sentries. "Put that in the hold for the journey."

One of the slug-troopers slithered towards Bart and grabbed him by the arm.

"But you said he could stay!" Niki objected. "That was our deal."

"Our deal was for the Leontine and the android," said Derek.

"That thing was never part of the agreement," said Pam, disgusted. "How could it be? It's just a meat-sack full of organs."

"You promised," said Niki frantically.

But the discussion was at an end and Pam and Derek were already turning to leave. Niki stared forlornly at

285

Bart, secured in the slimy arms of the slug-trooper.

"I'm sorry," she said.

Bart didn't speak, only glowered at her until the troopers began marching him out of the house.

"No!" yelled Sam, lunging to intercept them. He grabbed hold of Bart, trying to wrestle him from the trooper's grip. "You're not taking him." They fought briefly but then there was a searing blast of light and Sam crumpled to the floor. The trooper's colleague stood over him with his just-fired weapon.

Mercedes and Niki rushed to Sam's side. With a groan, he stirred and sat up.

"Bart…" he called out weakly.

"It's too late," said Mercedes. "He's gone."

Gathering themselves, the Apples and Gavin followed the others out of the house to watch the launch. Gavin froze at the sight of the hulking shape of the Lander in the moonlight. His legs, which had carried him this far, suddenly felt like cooked spaghetti.

"I don't do goodbyes," said a voice at his feet. He looked down to see Cupcake. "Unless they're of the terminal variety, of course."

"You're leaving too?"

"The League is giving me a lift back to the fleet and a new ship to replace the one that was destroyed. My

reward for helping them track down the princess. Sorry about that."

"That's OK," he said. "You were only doing your morally dubious job."

"Oh, I've been meaning to return this," said Cupcake. It was Gavin's journal.

"Hey, Earth Gavin, for a biped you're pretty nifty in a tight spot," said Cupcake. "Ever thought of becoming a bounty hunter?"

"Sure," he said. "Right after I've finished my astronaut training."

"I'm gonna miss that earthling sarcasm. Here, if you ever change your mind." Cupcake passed him what looked suspiciously like a squeaky plastic mouse toy.

"It's a squeaky plastic mouse toy," said Gavin.

"Don't be ridiculous. It's a hyperspace locator beacon. You need to code it to your personal identity. Press it three times."

SQUEAK! SQUEAK! SQUEAK!

"Next time you do that, wherever I am I'll get the message and know it's you." The cat threw him a salute. "Say bye to Tony for me. See you around, kid."

"See you, Cupcake."

With that the bounty hunter leapt up the ramp of the Lander and padded aboard without a backward glance.

Gavin stared down at the journal in his hand. He hadn't written anything in it about the Apples, not since discovering the truth about them. Not that a journal entry mattered – he was hardly going to forget the time that he lived next door to a family of aliens.

He dropped it into the backpack and slung the bag over his shoulder. "I'm never going to forget…"

"What did you say?" asked Sunshine Starburst at his side.

"Forget…" he repeated. "I think … I think…"

The Lander's engines fired up. Sam and Mercedes held one another tightly, watching Niki glide up the ramp to be swallowed by the darkness of the vessel's interior. Derek and Pam swept after her, their slug-troopers slithering behind them. The ramp began to retract.

Gavin's head, which had until then been clouded by gloomy goodbyes, was suddenly clear and laser focused.

"I think I know how to save her."

The hatch was closing.

It was now or never.

Grabbing Sunshine Starburst, he sprinted across the lawn. He was still wearing his dressing gown, with the plastic laser-sword tucked in the cord. It banged against his hip and the backpack full of glass dolphins clinked on his shoulders. He'd taken the precaution of clamping

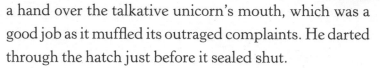

a hand over the talkative unicorn's mouth, which was a good job as it muffled its outraged complaints. He darted through the hatch just before it sealed shut.

He was inside the Lander – there was no turning back now. As he moved away from the entrance, he felt a tug at his hip. The closing hatch had nipped the hem of his dressing gown. He was stuck. From along the gangway came a wet squelch. With horror, Gavin saw that it was a slug-trooper. The bulbous creature filled the corridor, slime oozing between the plates of its combat armour, the sensory tentacles on its head twitching. It couldn't fail to notice him, except for one thing.

His cosmic ordinariness.

The trooper slid past him. Quickly, Gavin yanked free the trapped dressing gown.

"What have you done?!" Sunshine Starburst blurted, purple plastic heart beating wildly.

"Don't worry, I've got it all figured out."

"Oh, well then, that's completely fine." Sarcasm from a talking toy unicorn comes across as excessively bitter. "GET ME OFF THIS SH—"

Its cry was drowned out by a rumble from the atmospheric drive, and a second later the nose of the craft pitched up and they launched skyward. Gavin figured that even with his natural invisibility he had

to find somewhere to hide. Assuming that no one was likely to need a wee in the short time it would take to get from Earth to the orbiting flagship, he located a toilet. Locking the hatch behind him, he sat down on the closed lid of the toilet seat and grabbed a handhold. He noticed a porthole window. It was a loo with a view.

"I can see my house from here," he mumbled. By the time he got to the end of the sentence, the house, Middling and the whole country had dropped out of sight. The northern hemisphere receded below as they raced up through the atmosphere. He shifted position on the lid.

"Have you been yet?"

"What?"

"It's the toilet," explained Sunshine Starburst. "Quantum Flusher Mark Eight. Nag, nag, nag. Just ignore it."

"You'd better go before we leave the solar system," the toilet went on. "We're not stopping until we get there. And don't forget to lift the seat. It's electrified."

Sunshine Starburst wriggled out of his grip and pressed its nose up against the porthole. Gavin was aware of a shadow crossing the window and then the unicorn repeating the words, "Oh no, oh no, oh no…"

He leaned past it and squinted into space. The Lander

was travelling beneath another, much bigger ship, one that dwarfed even the Gastronite Magicruiser.

"Type 77 battleship," said Sunshine. "The most destructive force in the galaxy. D'Rek got it in the divorce."

As they flew on beneath the giant craft, Gavin recalled another passage from Derek's book.

✦

Forget space yachts or orbital battle stations, nothing says you've made it like a five-kilometre-long heavily armed battleship. I purchased my first from The Ultimate Killing Machine Corporation. Sleek and indestructible, it came in Stealth Black with Go-Faster-Than-Light stripes. I got a little carried away with the option list. So don't do what I did, and instead stick to these essentials: seat coverings made from the hides of your defeated enemies is always a good look; the Discomfort Pack is ideal if you're expecting to transport prisoners; and make sure it comes loaded with Android. Ideally, an army of killer androids.

✦

The sun edged over the superstructure. They were changing course. The Lander swung up and over the bigger ship, swooping low over sensor dishes, weapons turrets and a host of other stations whose function Gavin could only guess at. It had taken mere minutes to travel

from Middling to this point, but they flew across the surface of the ship for a long time before the note of the Lander's drive altered and its speed dropped. Ahead, the mighty flagship's giant hangar doors slowly drew apart. They edged inside and, with a series of clunks, Gavin felt the shuttle settle on its landing gear.

"What are we doing here?" asked Sunshine, the colours of its horn swirling wildly.

"I'm going to rescue the princess," said Gavin. "And quite possibly save the galaxy."

Chapter 32

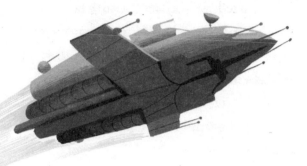

"Terrific," said the unicorn. "But did you have to schlep me along too?"

"Shh!" hissed Gavin. The Lander's outer hatch was opening. They waited in silence as Niki and the rest of the passengers and crew disembarked. Gavin could hear Cupcake asking for directions to its new ship, then Pam and Derek's smug, imperious tones, but nothing from Niki. He pictured her, quiet and furious.

"Tell me something," Sunshine asked. "Up until today what would you say is your greatest accomplishment?"

Gavin thought for a moment. "When I was ten, I collected a boatload of tokens from cereal packs to earn a

free trip to Legoland."

"Right, right." Sunshine Starburst nodded wisely. "You don't think saving the galaxy might be, how can I put this, a bit of a step up?"

"That's why I brought you," he said. "I figured you'd be able to help me by finding out where they're holding her. You just have to stick your horn into one of those sockets to access the ship's systems, right?"

"Oh sure, that'll do it. Easy. There, the galaxy is saved." The unicorn slapped a hoof to its head and groaned.

With the Lander now empty of crew, Gavin made his way to the open hatch and looked out over the vast hangar bay, lined with squadrons of sleek gunships. On the far side he spied a familiar figure. It was Cupcake, climbing aboard one of the craft. He didn't have to wait long before its drive fired up and the ship lifted off the deck. The craft angled towards a set of open hangar doors and flew out into space. Gavin knew he could call back the bounty hunter with three presses on the squeaky mouse toy, but as much as he wanted to, he daren't risk it. If the cat returned now it would draw suspicion and jeopardise his mission. This time he was on his own.

"OK, here goes." He crept across the bay, Sunshine trotting behind. They sneaked past the end of a row of fighters and their crews and slipped through a hatch into the passageway outside. He'd never felt happier at being so insignificant.

"There's one of those access points," he said, spotting it in the wall opposite. "Go on then, do your stuff."

Grumbling, Sunshine Starburst waddled over and inserted its horn. While it attempted to access the ship's systems, Gavin reflected that this was the fourth spaceship he'd been on in a month. The deck and walls were completely covered with deep-pile carpet in an avocado-green colour. From the ceiling at regular intervals dangled pendant lamps with bright-orange shades. And there was a lingering scent of orange spice throughout.

"What's with the funky decor?" he asked.

Sunshine Starburst's horn glowed as data streamed through it. "According to the onboard records, as soon as D'Rek got sole ownership of the flagship he planned on implementing a major upgrade to the weapons systems, navigational computers and interior design, but after the divorce he was extremely short of funds and had to abandon his plans. The ship hasn't been redecorated since it was commissioned in Galactic League Standard Year 1974. It's very fashionable, for the time."

"Attention, all crew." A ship-wide broadcast

interrupted the unicorn's report. "Prepare to make the jump to light speed in thirty minutes. That is three zero Galactic League minutes. Countdown to interstellar jump begins … now!"

On the carpeted bulkhead, and repeated the length of the passageway, appeared timers in squared-off glowing red digits, counting down from thirty minutes.

"Can you delay the jump?" asked Gavin.

"Doubtful. I'd have to talk to the flight systems and these Type 77s aren't known for their helpful attitude." Sunshine paused. "I've located the princess. Royal Suite, deck twelve."

Gavin picked up the unicorn and tucked it in the front fold of his dressing gown, facing out. He set off, flitting through the ship like a ghost, the deep-pile carpet deadening his footsteps and his stunningly unremarkable personality ensuring that he avoided the unwelcome attention of crew members and slug-troopers alike.

An elevator whisked them up to Niki's deck at the top of the ship. The doors opened on to a wide corridor with a bright-orange carpet, the walls covered in foil wallpaper, soft light spilling from teardrop-shaped pendants hanging along its length. Bland instrumental music drifted on the filtered air.

"Bossa nova," said Sunshine, tapping a hoof to the

rhythm, adding, "She's in there."

A set of highly decorated golden doors lay at the far end of the corridor, flanked by a pair of slug-sentries.

"How am I going to get past them?" At such close quarters, Gavin doubted even his ability to slip by without being spotted. He glanced at the wall where another countdown timer displayed the unwelcome information that in nineteen minutes the flagship would be leaving Earth orbit. He realised he was close enough to hear them chatting to one another.

"Hear what happened to Gary?"

"Gary from Interrogation?"

"No, Gary from Catering."

They continued to swap juicy slug gossip. It consisted mostly of a discussion about what they were going to have for dinner, which gave Gavin an idea.

"If only we had some lettuce," he said, "we could distract them."

"Maybe we do," said Sunshine. "Put me down."

He lowered the unicorn to the deck and it waddled to the nearest access node, inserting its horn in the slot. A moment later another ship's announcement sounded through the corridor.

"Attention, all crew."

It took Gavin a moment to recognise Sunshine's voice.

"To celebrate the glorious reunification of the Galactic League, all loyal subjects will receive an extra ration of slime mould and a complimentary sensory tentacle massage. This will be allocated on a deck-by-deck basis. Would all troopers on deck twelve please go *immediately* to the canteen to collect their reward."

The guards didn't need any more encouragement. They oozed off along the corridor, leaving glistening trails on the carpet. A pair of small, puck-shaped cleaning robots followed immediately behind them, mopping up.

Sunshine disconnected itself. "Shall we?" it said, padding towards the unguarded doors.

The Royal Suite was composed of several connected rooms, the first of which had a lofty ceiling, cork-covered walls and a sunken seating area. There was an L-shaped sofa in deep purple, a couple of leather beanbags and a chair that looked like a spherical basket suspended from the ceiling by a long, twined rope. Floor-standing lava lamps bubbled away, making swirling patterns and spilling orange and yellow light across the room. An open-tread, metal spiral staircase wound up to a landing, off which were doors that Gavin presumed led to the bedrooms.

"Niki?" he called.

"Oh dear, she's not here," said Sunshine Starburst

unconvincingly. "We should get off this ship and go home right away."

The basket-chair swung round, revealing Niki, legs curled up on the seat, immersed in her phone.

"Super," grumbled the unicorn.

"Gavin?!" Niki leapt up. "You changed your mind."

"About what?"

"Coming with me."

He'd almost forgotten about the invitation. "Uh … no. Sorry."

"Then what are you…?" Her puzzled gaze went from his face to the plastic laser-sword at his hip and back again. She winced. "Please don't say you're here to rescue me."

Before he could get a word out, she had spun him round and was marching him back towards the doors.

"You have to leave, right now."

"Listen to her," said Sunshine Starburst. "Wise words indeed."

"This ship's about to leave Earth orbit," she went on. "And if my parents catch you here—"

Gavin dug in his heels. "Wait! I have a plan to thwart them."

She put a hand on her hip. "*Thwart?* Really?"

"It was my journal that gave me the idea!"

"Gavin, stop! Whatever your plan is, it's not worth the risk. I'm not worth it. If I go back on my word to Pam and Derek they'll destroy Earth. You earthlings may be ordinary, but some of you are special to me." She paused. "I'd rather spend the rest of my life as a rotten galactic princess than be responsible for your planet's destruction. And anyway, there's nothing for me back there, not after what I said. Sam and Mercedes must hate me."

"No they don't," he said. "I mean, I thought they did too, but I was wrong. Just like I was wrong about Nan and Grandad. I thought they were sending me away, but actually they were turning the attic into another bedroom. See?"

"Um, not really."

He tried again. "Families. They're not a competition, whatever Pam and Derek might think. Sam, Mercedes and Bart are your people. You can't win or lose their love; it's just there all the time. They'll always make room for you."

Niki considered his speech. "Still not entirely sure how an attic conversion fits into all this, but I get the gist." She paused. "Thanks, Gavin."

"Attention, all crew," boomed another announcement. "Fifteen minutes until interstellar jump."

As the message faded there was a small sound from the door to the suite.

"Someone's outside," squealed Sunshine.

The door handles dipped. Whoever it was, they were coming in.

Chapter 33

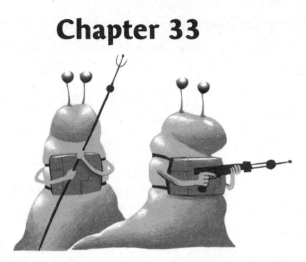

"Quick," said Niki, pushing Gavin towards the spiral staircase. He snatched Sunshine Starburst and scampered up to the landing just as the gilded entrance doors swung open and in strutted Pam and Derek. At their side marched a couple of heavily armed, extra-large slug-troopers in highly polished white armour. Gavin crouched behind the banister and watched them.

"Where are your guards?" asked Derek.

Niki was sitting on the purple sofa, pretending to be absorbed in her painted fingernails. She gave a non-committal shrug.

"Dereliction of duty," he said. "Remind me to have

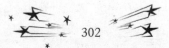

them sent to the salt mines."

On the landing, Gavin was aware of Sunshine Starburst trembling beside him. Mindless fear set off its speech synthesiser and the unicorn announced loudly, "Be my best friend!"

"What was that?" Pam turned her gimlet stare on the landing. "Is someone there?"

"Only me," said a voice from over Gavin's shoulder.

He turned to see Bart emerging from one of the bedrooms – Niki must have persuaded her parents not to stick him in the hold for the journey. Bart winked at him as he trotted downstairs.

Ignoring Bart, Pam beamed at Niki and Derek. "Look at us all back together again, a normal, happy family. I thought this afternoon we could go for ice cream, then inflict some galaxy-wide misery."

"Sounds perfect; we should take a picnic," said Derek. He snapped his fingers. "Sorry, I don't mean picnic, I mean Trans-Warp Cluster Apocalypse Torpedo."

"Ten minutes until interstellar jump," came another announcement.

Niki tore her eyes away from her nail varnish. "I'd like to remain in orbit a while longer. I want to see the sun rise over the Earth one more time."

Gavin knew she didn't care about the view; she was

trying to buy him more time to leave the ship.

"How amusing that you should request one *last* look,"
Derek said with a smirk. "Since the planet will shortly
cease to exist."

Niki sat bolt upright. "No! You promised. You said if I
came with you then you'd leave it alone."

"Oh, come now, you never really believed that,
hatchling," said Pam, stroking Niki's cheek with her
long fingers.

"Earthlings harboured you," said Derek. "And for
that they must be made an example of."

Pam fiddled with a blue and white earring. "And their
planet will make a fine match for this one."

Gavin felt a hot surge of anger. They were going to
shrink the Earth after all, wiping out everyone he knew
and loved. He was the wrong boy in the wrong place at
the wrong time. But his moment had come. He leapt to
his feet.

"Get down! They'll see you!" hissed Sunshine.

Ignoring the unicorn's pleas, he unleashed what he
hoped was a fearsome battle-cry and charged down the
stairs to confront Pam, Derek and destiny.

Turns out it's not so easy to charge down a spiral
staircase. The twisty bits make it really hard to build up
a head of steam, so by the time he hit the bottom step his

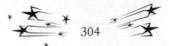

battle-cry had dwindled to a half-hearted mumble and everyone in the room was staring at him.

"Gavin," said Niki tensely. "Not the moment."

"It's OK," he said, fumbling in the backpack. "I'm armed and dangerous."

"Who is this?" asked Pam, flicking a dismissive finger in his direction.

He stopped rummaging. "Oh, come on. We literally just spent the last month together. It's me, Gavin, remember?"

Pam and Derek conferred with each other, but it was clear from their empty shrugs that he had slipped from their memories.

"Detain the Gavin," Pam coolly instructed her guards.

They slithered towards him, weapons pointed at his head. He dug a hand deeper into the bag, and among the coloured glass dolphins his fingers touched the welcome spike of bristles.

"Back off!" he barked, whipping out the electric toothbrush. The guards paused mid-slither. Emboldened by their reaction, he poked the device at them. "Yeah, you don't like that, do you? Huh? Huh?"

The plan had come to him when Cupcake returned his journal, the moment he realised that Niki was ... "Unforgettable," he said aloud.

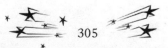

"What?" said Pam sharply.

"I think it's broken," said Derek.

"What if I could make you forget about her? What if I could make her so cosmically insignificant that you would leave her to live her life with the people who really care for her?"

With a shaking hand, he sank his thumb against the toothbrush's power button. There was a buzzing sound, the compact head spun for a second, and stopped. Had it worked? He glanced across at Niki and Bart, who were both sporting pained expressions. That would be a no then.

Gavin realised he was in big trouble.

He mashed the button again. Nothing. And then he noticed a red flashing light at the base of the handle.

"Out of charge," he mumbled.

"Take him!" commanded Pam.

He felt the slimy hands of the first guard grip him. The second snatched the toothbrush. He was too shaken to put up any kind of resistance. His last-ditch plan had ended up in a ditch.

"Don't hurt him!" Niki pleaded, and her lip curled into a cruel smile. "Let *me*."

Uh, hello? *What* did she just say?

Pam and Derek beamed at their daughter. Sam had

warned him that Niki would change, that she would follow the dark path trodden by her parents. He just hadn't expected her to skip along it so readily.

"Pathetic human," she hissed. "You dared to oppose the might of the Galactic League." She threw back her head and laughed. "Soon you will witness its ultimate power. Let my first act as Supreme Monarch be ... to destroy Earth."

Chapter 34

Gavin didn't believe it, even if Pam and Derek were lapping up their hatchling's newly minted attitude. It was a ploy – had to be. Niki was only *acting* the evil princess, pretending to be on her parents' side. At least, he was fairly confident she was acting. He'd only seen her in the school production of *Fiddler on the Roof*, so unless she suddenly burst into song, he couldn't be sure.

Pam and Derek swept out of the suite with Niki between them and Bart trailing obediently behind. Gavin glanced up to the landing, where Sunshine Starburst cowered in terror, and couldn't help but think that the unicorn's fears of a horror story in space were

coming true.

"March, Earth scum." One of the slug-troopers prodded him in the back with its rifle, and he stumbled after the royal entourage.

"Take him to the cells," commanded Pam.

"Please, Mother," said Niki in a wheedling voice. "Surely it would be crueller to force the earthling to witness the destruction of his homeworld?"

"Oh, hatchling," cooed Pam. "It is good to have you back."

Acting. It was just acting. So why, Gavin wondered, did he just feel his faith in Niki wobble?

They made their way to the command bridge on the topmost deck of the ship. Elevator doors opened on to a large circular room arranged with individual stations for navigation, weaponry and communications. Each station featured a screen set into a freestanding cabinet made from polished walnut. Crew members sat in front of their stations in chairs with chromed tubular frames and black leather seat-pads. Instead of a carpet there were individual floor mats at each station and scattered around the deck were several knotted rugs in earth tones featuring geometric designs. They looked like trip hazards to Gavin. Light came from anglepoise lamps at each station and a single great chandelier hanging from

the central portion of the domed ceiling. The whole place smelled of pine air freshener.

The bridge crew were neither robots nor slugs, but instead resembled octopuses, their multiple tentacles tapping and swiping the complex controls on each console. All of the crew faced a large, central viewscreen at the front of the room, which displayed a live image of the Earth.

There was a pair of command thrones in the centre of the bridge. Pam slid into one and Derek plumped down in the other. Bart fell in a respectful few strides behind, while Niki took up a position beside the thrones, hands clasped behind her back. The slug-trooper steered Gavin next to her.

"Princess, you have control," said Derek with a wave, passing responsibility for the attack to her.

"Thank you, Father. Power up the Diminisher," she commanded.

"Aye, aye, Princess," gurgled the octopus in charge of the weapon.

Niki quickly looked over and gave Gavin a wink. The wink said to him that she had a plan, that all was not lost and with a bit of luck they'd prevent Earth from being turned into a bauble. At least, he hoped it was a wink, but it could just as easily have been a piece of grit in her

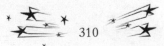

eye. He had to admit, he was putting a lot of faith in a single eyelid.

"Use your sword," she whispered.

At least that confirmed she was pretending, but didn't she realise it was a toy? Even if it had been real, he was hardly going to fence their way out of here.

"Batteries," she mouthed.

His hand fell on to the hilt and he remembered that he'd loaded it with fresh ones before going to the party. Furtively he located the battery compartment. The cover flipped off with a click he was sure one of the guards must have heard. He held his breath. Seconds passed and there was no rifle in the back. He'd got away with it. Heart racing, he looked down.

Double As!

He emptied two of the precious batteries into his palm. Niki gave the tiniest of nods.

Now all they had to do was get them into the toothbrush.

Unaware of its importance, the slug-trooper who had confiscated it in the Royal Suite had tucked the device loosely in the pouch of an ammo belt wrapped around his bulging middle. The neck and bristled head poked out invitingly. Gavin reached out a hand, but as he edged closer to the toothbrush, Pam's voice cut across.

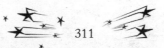

"Give the earthling a better view," she purred.

The other trooper pinned his arms and steered him to a spot almost directly beneath the giant viewscreen. With each footstep the Neural-B and the batteries grew further apart. It was hopeless.

"That will do," said Pam. "From there you may even be able to hear your species' final anguished cries." She laughed and Derek patted her hand affectionately.

"My dearest, I had forgotten just how warped you can be." Derek's hair ignited with affection.

Gavin was so close to the screen he couldn't see its edges. Earth filled his vision. They were currently in orbit above the northern hemisphere. He could make out a massive electrical storm rolling in over continental Europe, and clusters of man-made lights marking out the major cities. The world spun on, seven and a half billion inhabitants unaware how close they were to being shrunk out of existence. Maybe it was a good thing they didn't know what was about to hit them. He knew he should feel bad for everyone, but the only people he could think about were Nan, Grandad and the Tiny Horror, back in his little street in Middling.

"The Diminisher is ready to fire, Your Highness," confirmed the weapons octopus.

Middling!

The town was the most overlooked on the planet, possibly the most boring place in the galaxy – and it might just be Earth's last chance.

Gavin spun round, so that the planet loomed behind him and it was as if he was talking for all humankind.

"In eighteen ninety-two, Middling's first shoe factory was established, producing leather sandals primarily for the burgeoning export market."

Pam and Derek regarded him with quizzical expressions.

"Local Middling resident Arthur Creech is widely credited as being the first person to establish that it is impossible to lick your own elbow."

One of Derek's eyelids drooped, and his fiery hair burned lower. Pam yawned and mashed her lips together. Bart attempted to lick his own elbow.

As Gavin proceeded to recount facts about Middling's extensive CCTV camera network, the hundred-year losing streak of its local football team, and details of the residents' parking scheme, Pam, Derek and the octopus crew were lulled into a stupor. Just as he'd hoped.

Niki made her move.

Swiping the toothbrush from the slug-trooper's belt and clamping it between her teeth, she stepped up on

to one arm of her mother's throne and launched herself off. Catching the chandelier with both hands, she swung across the deck over the heads of the gawping crew to make a perfect two-footed landing next to Gavin. Emptying the useless batteries with a shake of her hand, she thrust it at him.

"You could've just thrown it," he said.

"Would you have caught it?"

"Fair point." He shoved the first battery into the empty compartment.

"Reverse the polarity of the electron flow!" yelled Niki.

"Huh?"

She stabbed a finger at the battery. "Wrong way!"

Swiftly correcting the position of the positive and negative poles, he inserted the second battery.

Pam and Derek were coming out of their daze and rapidly figuring out that all was not going according to plan. Their plan, anyway. Worst of all, their perfect princess had duped them both.

"Stop them!" Pam screeched.

With a slithering snap, the slug-troopers levelled their weapons. Waving their rubbery tentacles and belching clouds of black ink in panic, the octopus crew dived for cover. In the chaos, one of them tripped over the corner

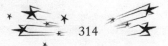

of a rug.

Niki whipped off her tiara and, wielding it like a boomerang, hurled it across the bridge. It flew swift and true, clattering into the barrel of the first trooper's rifle and knocking it aside to spoil his aim. The fizzing bolt flew well wide of Gavin. He heard the sizzle of the second gun firing, and a grunt of pain. He checked himself for an injury. No holes. Niki was in one piece too.

"Fire the Diminisher!" Derek yelled.

"Sire, the ship's systems are not responding," reported one brave octopus who had remained at his post. "It appears we have been locked out."

Derek stood bolt upright. "Impossible!" he bellowed. "What could possibly overpower a Type 77 battleship?"

The viewscreen flickered and the image of Earth vanished, to be replaced by an animated rainbow that sprang across the display, accompanied by a tinkling piece of music that was deeply annoying even on first hearing. Sunshine Starburst's face zoomed in to fill the screen.

"Hi, I'm Sunshine Starburst, your unicorn buddy," it chirped. "This flagship is now under the control of me and my magical friends: Happy Snowflake, Twilight Ruby and Barry Sutton. You can kiss my rainbow—"

"Assault troops to the bridge!" yelled Derek, but it

was too late.

"Now!" cried Niki.

Gavin lifted the toothbrush, aimed it at Pam and Derek – and fired.

A cone of mint-green light leapt from the buzzing head, enveloping the rulers of the galaxy. The device drained the batteries in a matter of seconds and the cone faded almost as quickly as it had appeared. Gavin held his breath, waiting to discover if the memory erasure had worked.

Pamnatakrocula the Pitiless and D'Rek the Destroyer stirred as if from a deep sleep. The first thing they set eyes on was each other.

"Pam?" said Derek.

"Derek?" said Pam.

They looked around them, mystified at their surroundings.

"Is this Middling?" asked Derek.

"I think it's the new department store," replied Pam.

"Yes!" Gavin said under his breath, pumping a fist in delight. Against all hope and most reasonable expectation, his plan had worked. He turned to Niki, but she was already on the move. A terrible expression clouded her face.

"Bart," she whispered.

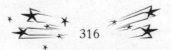

316

He lay sprawled on the deck next to the throne, unmoving, a wisp of smoke rising from a pinpoint blast-hole in his chest.

Chapter 35

Niki crouched by Bart's prone body. He was still breathing, but barely.

"What happened to him?" asked Gavin.

"When the slug-troopers opened fire, I deflected the shot meant for you," she said. "Bart must've thrown himself in front of the blaster aimed at me." He was trying to say something, his words coming in ragged breaths. "Don't try to speak," she said.

"It's OK," he said, gazing up at her. "I was born to save you."

"Not like this, you muppet."

His brow creased. "What's a muppet?"

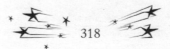

"I believe it's an Earth insult among siblings," she said. "At school when Lianne Cohen's brother changed all the contact names in her phone to seventeenth-century astronomer Johannes Kepler, that's what she called him."

The effort of even this short conversation was too much for Bart and he sank into unconsciousness. But just before he did a smile flickered across his lips and happily he mumbled the words, "Sibling insult…"

"Take him to the medical bay," Niki ordered. The octopus and slug-trooper crew members hesitated, looking to Pam and Derek for their instructions. Unfortunately for the crew, their former masters were currently wandering the bridge like a couple of tourists, asking for directions to Men's Fashion. Niki stood up and repeated the order, with her hair flaming. This time the crew tripped over themselves to obey. Bart was whisked away, and over the next two hours the ship's medical staff managed to stabilise him, but his condition remained critical.

"What do we do now?" Gavin said as they sat vigil by his sickbed.

Niki laid her hand on his. "We need to get him home."

◆

Sunshine Starburst piloted the Imperial Lander back

to Middling. In the cockpit Niki and Gavin could only watch as machines kept Bart alive, his vital signs weakening with every passing minute. Dawn was coming up as they touched down in the Apples' back garden. They'd sent a message about their arrival, so Sam and Mercedes were waiting even as the ramp descended. They transferred Bart to the home office, and then to the secret underground room. Mercedes carried out a series of scans and informed them of her findings.

"The blast from the weapon has fatally compromised his heart. Even if I could fabricate a new one, he will expire before it is ready to implant."

A dreadful silence fell over the room, and then Niki spoke up.

"What about a transplant? Bart was born to be a perfect donor for me. Which means I can be *his* donor, right? I have two hearts – he can have one of mine."

Mercedes and Sam exchanged a confused look, and then Sam said, "Your Highness, why would you do such a thing?"

Gavin could see Niki's mind working. She was finally reaching the same understanding that he had come to some time ago.

"Because he's my brother."

Some families you were born with; some took shape

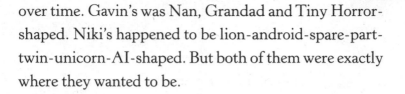

over time. Gavin's was Nan, Grandad and Tiny Horror-shaped. Niki's happened to be lion-android-spare-part-twin-unicorn-AI-shaped. But both of them were exactly where they wanted to be.

✦

It was a few weeks later when Sam invited Gavin over to his home office for a chat. Sam clapped him on the back with a hefty paw, almost knocking him over. Gavin sat down, noticing a pot of tea and a jam sponge on the desk, next to a vicious-looking cake knife.

"Going after Niki like that, you were either very brave, or you had no idea what you were getting into." He poured them both a cup of tea. "On my homeworld we honour those of exceptional courage."

"Do I get a medal?" Gavin asked, taking a sip. He wouldn't have objected to a medal.

"Sort of," said Sam, picking up the knife next to the cake. "It is a symbol, etched in your skin, drawn in blood."

"That's not a cake knife, is it?"

Sam laughed. The blade shone in the sunlight streaming through the window. "Now where would you like it? The hind quarters are customary."

Gavin swallowed his tea with a gulp. Just then there was a rap on the window. It was Niki. Seeing her, Gavin

quickly made an excuse and left.

"Thanks for that," he said as they crossed the lawn. "I think I was about to get my bum inscribed."

"It's a great honour. Sam must really like you."

Mercedes was tending to her flower border. She looked serenely happy as she dug holes and filled them with seeds. "Staying for lunch, Gavin? It's Nutella with cucumber and then baked bean ice lollies."

"She still hasn't quite got the hang of earthling food," muttered Niki.

They sat on the wall outside the house, kicking their heels. It was only then that Gavin noticed Niki's T-shirt. This one was decorated with the words "Galactic Princess".

"Isn't that a bit of a giveaway?"

"Who's going to believe a galactic princess lives here?"

She had a point. The front door opened and Bart emerged in his tracksuit, heading out for a run. He performed a few stretches before setting off. The operation had been a complete success. Gavin wondered if some of Niki's personality had been transplanted along with the organ, because following the procedure she and Bart had started behaving like any other siblings, trading the vilest insults and complaining loudly to Sam and Mercedes when they felt the other was receiving more

than his or her fair share of screen-time/cake/attention.

"Hi, neighbour," Gavin called to him.

He grunted in reply. Bart was less cheery since his transplant – possibly another consequence of Niki's organ donation – which frankly came as something of a relief.

"Here," he said, handing his sister a book. "Next time get it yourself. I'm not your slave."

She took it and he jogged off. As he went one way along the street, from the other came Derek on his bike. He whooshed past, a blur of clashing Lycra.

"Lovely day for it," he called out, giving them a friendly wave.

"So weird," Gavin mumbled. "I'm never going to get used to that."

"If you think that's strange," said Niki, "Pam's the new yoga instructor at the leisure centre."

After a family meeting, the Apples had decided that even though Pam and Derek no longer remembered their past lives it was too risky to send them away with the Galactic League fleet. Out there in the cosmos there was a chance they could be restored to their former evil selves. There was only one way to ensure the continued safety of Niki and planet Earth. Which is how the rulers of the galaxy ended up moving back into number forty-

six Park Street, Middling.

Gavin turned to Niki. "If Pam and Derek are out of the galactic despot business, then technically aren't you in charge now?"

She ran a finger across her T-shirt, underlining the words. "Yup."

"How are you going to manage that? I mean – can you rule the galaxy and keep on top of your schoolwork?"

"I might have to give up one or two extracurricular activities. But not the orchestra. Or chess. Or taekwondo. Obviously."

"Obviously."

She lifted the book and stared at the cover. Gavin balked, knowing what lay within its pages.

"You're not going to use that, are you?"

"Course not. It's my dad's idea of how to run things." She turned to the inside page and the dedication, which was to her. "Pam and Derek have left the galaxy in a mess. All that fighting between them has caused chaos and division. I reckon it's my responsibility to restore peace." She looked up. "Want to help?"

Nan and Grandad had already started work on his new room – he wasn't about to move to the Galactic League's homeworld. "I can't leave now. I'm sorry."

"Who said anything about leaving?"

He almost fell off the wall. "You want to rule the galaxy ... from Middling?"

"Why not? And while we're at it, we need a new guidebook. This one's full of terrible advice. What the galaxy needs is something that combines dazzling and marvellous insight – provided by *me* – with more down-to-earth, ordinary suggestions. *Cosmically* ordinary..."

"You want *me* to help you write a new guide?"

"Obviously my name comes first on the cover."

"Goes without saying."

"So you're in?"

It was a lot to absorb. "Can I think about it?"

"Sure. Take your time," she said, fidgeting with the book. "Galactic rulers are famously known for their *incredible* patience. Yup. My middle name is Empress Laid Back. Easy-going, that's me. *Nonchalant*. So, have you thought about it yet?"

He didn't answer immediately, and in the brief silence he was aware of all too familiar music coming from Niki's open bedroom window.

"Uh, when exactly are you going to let them go?"

She shrugged – the fate of Cubic Parsec was so not important right now. "Well?"

"I've thought about it," said Gavin.

She raised her eyebrows in anticipation and he shot

her a grin. "I'm in."

A smile slid across Niki's face. "Good decision." She held out the book and, with a heave, tossed it over her shoulder.

"Middling is about to become the centre of the galaxy."

Tyrant Feedback Form

We want you to be completely satisfied with your experience of being despotically ruled over. Fill out this form to let us know how we could improve our unforgiving regime.

And remember: A Happy Downtrodden Population Is … Definitely Not Our Priority.

1. How would you describe yourself?

a. You wouldn't. That's how you come to the notice of the Secret Police.

b. Previously oppressed.

c. Completely satisfied with your crushing existence.

2. How did you choose our service?

a. Evil Search Engine.

b. Saw our ad in *Best Small Dictators of the Galaxy* magazine.

c. There was a choice? You woke up one morning to find a battle fleet in orbit around your homeworld.

3. *What are your main concerns about being tyrannically oppressed?*
a. The compulsory uniforms are a bit itchy.
b. Your favourite TV show was cancelled.
c. A thousand years of relentless subjugation.

4. *What, if anything, is stopping you from overthrowing our rule?*
a. You couldn't fit it in between mandatory rock-breaking and slaving in the uranium mines.
b. Our informants are everywhere. Yes, even your goldfish is working for us.
c. The Orbital Armageddon Doom Blaster pointed at your planet.

5. *How likely are you to recommend us to another peaceful, unsuspecting planet? Answer this question using Despairing Screams.*
a. AAGH!
b. AAAAAAGH!
c. AAAAAAAAAGH!

6. *What do you like least about The Supreme Leader?*
a. This is a trick question.
b. No, really, I wouldn't answer if I were you.
c. Seriously, big mistake.
d. On the upside, it would be the very last mistake you ever make.

Thank you for taking the time to complete the questionnaire. Based on your answers you can expect a knock on the door from the Secret Police and immediate transport to Desolation Rock Prison Planet.